ULTIMATE SECRETS

By: Neil Feeney

Reviewed By: A. Feeney, S. Feeney, Maryjo Gorney, and Rachel Jones

Acknowledgments

I feel I owe a lot to everyone in my life, for not only helping me but loving me and giving me hope throughout my life. Included in that are my parents, who have raised me and loved me throughout school, home, and life, my friends who have continued to help me through this 'mental unbalanced'-ness and, well, everything. And last but most defiantly not least, are all of my teachers in my life. They have continually put up with me and taught me about everything from math to history to science, and even encouraged me to write this novel.

Oh, and a little shout-out to the best band in the world, Muse.

-Neil Feeney

Chapter One

"Ok guys listen up!" Mark told us.

"Oh what now?" Luke said sadly.

"What's that? You listen here mother skupper. We're gonna win this game. And we'll do it with or without you." Mark yelled at Luke. That got Luke's attention.

"Just throw the pull, Mark. We all know what we're doing." I said, and was rewarded by cheers by the team.

"Only one way to find out, Melvin. Let's do this." Mark said and raised the frisbee (or the disc as we call it) into the air. The other team across the field raised their hands, almost in unison. Mark released his backhand and the frisbee went into the air and straight toward the other team.

Ultimate Frisbee is a simple game. There are two teams of even numbers. Once a team has the disc, they throw it to each of their team members, much like soccer. Only in this game, once you have the disc you can only pivot one foot, no moving. The goal is to throw the disc to one of your teammates inside the end zone. Once caught, the team gets a point, then "pulls" (or throws) the disc to the other team, who has aligned themselves on the end zone on the other side of the field. If the disc is dropped or intercepted by the other team, the opposing team gets the disc and throws to each of their teammates to the opposite end zone.

We ran toward the other team. I stopped, as I realized that the person I was covering (the person who I would defend from the other team) didn't stop like the rest of his teammates, but kept running. That little skupper was going to the end zone! I won't let the team throw a long one just to get this point over with! I quickly ran into pursuit.

"Melvin!" I heard John yell as I ran. I risked a look behind me as I ran. I was right. The other team threw a bomb and the frisbee was heading directly toward the end zone. I looked ahead again. The opposing member was far ahead of me.

This is a great time to let the tension grow as I explain my team (or at least the names). There's Mark,

John, Luke, Bill, Doug, Frank, and Jake. The dream team. Our team name is "The Musers", that's because of the best band in the world, Muse. Since teams this year were only supposed to have no more than eight, the fields were around seventy yards long and around twenty wide.

I quickly ran, and ran, and ran. My cleats picked up shards of grass and dirt and threw it behind me. I could see that the runner in front of me was doing the same. I could hear the disc approaching, cutting the wind. The runner in front stopped in the end zone and turned, waiting for the disc to drop into his hands. I wasn't gonna get there in time. I wasn't, there's no possible way, and I was already a good ten yards away. I picked up a good burst of speed from inside and closed the distance between us. I saw the disc breeze my right shoulder as I dove. My feet left the air and I flew for a couple feet before smacking down the disc before it met my enemy's hands. My sweet victory was ended with a hard collision with the ground. I managed to curl myself into sort of a half-ball as I hit the ground. Pain hit, but it wasn't too bad. I've had worse.

I jumped back up and grabbed the disc off the ground. I brushed it off, and then walked to the front side of my runner buddy. I held out the disc for him to tap. Once he tapped it the game was in play.

"Disc is in!" I yelled and quickly looked for a teammate to throw to. The other man was yelling the stall count at me. The stall count is the 10 seconds that we get to throw the disc, or the other team gets it.

I saw Bill start sprinting toward me, his defender far behind him -- smart man, making an in cut. I made the familiar two-finger peace sign under the disc, getting ready to throw a forehand. Forehands are throwing with your right hand, and backhands are with your left hand.

I faked a backhand and as my defender threw himself to defend the fake; I flicked a forehand to Bill. He caught it and I ran across the soccer field we were on. I saw Bill throw a quick backhand to Doug. I picked up the pace. One of Doug's favorite things to do is throw long ones.

"Melvin!" I heard Doug yell. Yep, he was throwing a bomber. I could almost hear him release the powerful backhand and let the disc go flying. When I reached the end zone I barely had any time to recover from the run across the field. I could see above me that the disc was hovering and slowly making its way to above me. I jumped up with both hands to catch the disc, but I felt my defenders' hands smack it out of the air and to the ground.

"Skup!" I said to myself as the man from the other team picked it up and faced me, disc out.

"Disc is in!" he shouted as I tapped it in.

"Stall one, stall two." Before I could finish he threw a quick forehand to one of his teammates that was uncovered.

I looked and saw that Luke was walking halfway into the field, and was letting his defender open.

"Come on Luke!" I screamed as I followed my defender as he ran back. My defender stopped, then started running behind me. I wouldn't let him get this in cut. I stopped, and then followed him. The member with the disc threw it straight to my defender, but I was there to smack it down.

I picked it up and threw it to Mark before my defender could even begin the stall count. Once the disc left my hands I was already running. Mark caught the disc, and then once his defender started the stall, he threw it to Bill. Bill caught it then flicked it to Luke. I could see that something was wrong with Luke; he didn't seem, well, into it. He tried to catch it but it fell right out of his hands.

"Turn!" someone from the other team called. That meant that the other team had the disc.

"Luke!" I yelled at him. He shrugged. With the other team winning 3-1, we can't have Luke make these stupid mistakes. My defender was doing all the tricks in the book -- fakes, turns, cuts-- but I stayed on his tale. I don't care if his whole team is passing the disc to one another; I won't let the person I'm covering get it.

But with me to the right, and my defender to the left, he made a dirty move. He cut straight in front of me, forcing me to stop while he just ran the other way.

"No skupping way!" I grunted and sprinted to follow him. He already had the in cut all worked out, and one of his teammates threw him the disc. He caught it and I was there in a second to start the stall. This time I was angry, I would let him get this throw out. I watched his eyes very carefully. They flickered from left to right, and my attention was split three ways.

One, I was keeping track out loud of the stall. Two, I was watching his eyes, waiting for them the light up as he found someone to throw to. And three, I was watching his entire body, when he curved his body to the right for a forehand; I was there right in front to block that chance. I heard him grunt every time I blocked it, and I could feel his teammates running behind me trying to get open, but I could sense that my teammates were giving no mercy as well.

"Eight!" the person I was covering yelled, telling his team that he was on stall eight. I continued to nine, and then right before the word "ten" came out of my mouth he threw a backhand. A weak attempt to get the disc as far away from our end zone as possible. I flung out my hand and felt the disc slam into it.

"Thanks." I said, smiling as I picked the disc off the ground and had my defender tap it in. I frantically looked for someone to throw to. I felt my defender's eyes on mine; he was using the same idea. I saw Frank attempt an in cut, but his defender was already there. I searched around some more. I saw Jake make a cut to where Frank just was, so I faked a forehand and threw him a backhand.

Jake caught it and turned, scanning the field for a worthy member to pass it to. I realized that my opponent was far behind me.

"Back!" I yelled and Jake threw the disc a couple of feet in front of me, I caught it and stopped as my defender caught up and started the stall. I didn't let him get the advantage. I flicked it to Mark as he ran behind me.

Mark's defender smacked the disc forward, a couple of yards in front of them. Mark dove and caught the disc with one hand and smashed into the ground. I could hear our team at various places across the field cheer. Mark jumped up and quickly flicked it to me. Before I even caught it I saw my defender approaching. I slammed my back to stop him as I caught the disc. I saw out of the corner of my eye that Doug was running long.

"DOUG!!!" I screamed as I flung out a backhand.

"HUH?" I heard Doug scream as he stopped in the end zone and turned around. It was then that I realized that I threw it too high. I stood there, staring, hoping that Doug could jump. But as I watched, I saw that his defender was quickly approaching. As the disc approached him, I saw him jump. He jumped too early; he wouldn't be able to get it.

Doug realized I was right as he started to fall back down to earth as the disc went above him. They were about to collide, however the disc would go right over his head. But then his right hand flung up, and snatched it out of the sky. I heard his defender grunt and start to jog back to his end zone. Doug started a little celebration dance as I ran over to join him. I felt my team behind me.

"Good job Doug!" We all told him one at a time.

"Come on guys! Three to two's not bad! Let's finish this baby up! First to five wins!" Frank called out.

"Let's win it!" I yelled. My team cheered.

We eventually lost the game.

After the game we all traveled to our cars and drove over to Exo-Politics, the pub where we always meet after every game. On the drive over I looked at myself in the rearview mirror. I had a bit of dried blood on my nose, no doubt from the diving I did. I had a simple face, short blonde hair and glasses, which I guess is normal for my age of twenty-three. I still had my Musers uniform on, with our team colors, orange and white, covering the front with "MUSERS" in big letters. Our team wears it to the pub after every game. Call it team spirit.

I parked and started down the brick walkway to the entrance. I saw Steve and Bob, two friends, outside the pub on one of the picnic tables with beers in hand.

"How was the game?" Steve called out.

"We lost five to three." I said back.

"Shame." Bob remarked.

"See ya inside." Steve said.

"See ya." I responded. I pushed open the big wooden doors and was greeted with a warm atmosphere with light lighting and a bar in the back corner, with tables scattered, and rock music blasting. I sat down at the one where all my mates were, and everyone was wearing their uniforms. I sat down, and I saw that my entire team was here.

A waitress walked over.

"How was the game?" She asked.

"Well, we lost, but we had a fun time." Frank said.

"Great." She said then started to walk away.

"Gloria!" Doug called out.

"Ya hon?" Gloria replied.

"Get us some beers on me." Doug said, and was rewarded by cheers and slaps on the back.

"You betcha!" Gloria said then hurried off. With long black hair and pretty blue eyes, she didn't look too bad this evening.

I smiled and looked around the table. Each one of my teammates was talking to another, engaged in what they were saying. I looked at each one.

Frank had long blond hair, tightened in a pony tail in the back with lumpy cheeks. Mark had short black hair, almost making him look bald, with a heavy frame. Doug on the other hand, was muscular with a great smile and longer black hair. Luke was the next one, with a smile and scruffy looking red dyed hair. Bill had glasses, with scruffy looking black hair. I looked over to John. He had a combed back strawberry blonde hair, but it was all messed up from the game. And finally there was Jake, who wore a baseball cap (that had the MUSE logo of course) to cover up his black hair. This was my family.

"Oi! Melvin!" I turned to see Frank, who was sitting next to me.

"Yep?" I asked, turning around.

"We were thinking about a new game plan for Saturday's game." He responded.

"Awesome! What is it?" I said back as Gloria came over with the beers. I was now engaged in the talking. I didn't even notice the cold faces behind skeleton masks watching me from their car outside.

Three hours later, I walked (or maybe jogged) over to the bathroom. I hardly noticed the two men with the masks standing outside the door. As I ran in, one of the men caught the door and the two ran in after me.

When I was finished, I walked over to wash my hands. In the mirror there was nothing. I leaned down and watched the germs get wiped off my hands and listened to the music played in the speakers overhead. But then when I leaned back up, the two men with masks were reflected in the mirror behind me.

"Guys, you know the rules...no masks in the pub." I said, annoyed, and then started to walk away. One of them stuck out his hand.

"You're not going anywhere." He said with a graveled voice. I scanned the room. The only thing I could see that I could defend myself with was the soap dispenser, one of those brand bottles. I grabbed that with my free hand and threw it at the man's face. He let go out of surprise and I ran out of the bathroom. When the door closed behind me I reached for the chair next to the door (ya know, those random chairs that no one knows why they're there) and stuck it under the knob. They won't be getting out for a while.

On the walk back to the table I met up with Gloria.

"Hey, there are a couple of guys in the bathroom messing up the place." I said, and I think I got the point across.

"I'm on it." Gloria said then started to walk away.

"Oh, and Gloria?" I said.

"Yep?" She turned around. I thought about it.

"Never mind." I said then walked away. I didn't have the guts to ask her out. And I never would. Maybe it's my name (what kind of name is Melvin?), or my hair, but I don't think girls really like me. I've always not really liked my hair, that's why I dyed it from brown to blonde. Now it kind of looks weird, but I like it. It's unique.

I walked back to the table. Once I sat down, Frank started talking.

"Did you ask Gloria out?" he asked.

"Where would you get that idea from?" I shot back.

"Well you're always looking at her." He said. He had a point. But I decided to lie.

"That's not true. No one knows it." I said.

"Really? Who here thinks that Melvin should ask Gloria out?" Frank asked the table.

"Yep."

"Mmmmmmmmmhmm."

"You betcha."

"Ah, shut up!" I yelled at the group and took another swig of beer. Everybody laughed.

"You sure, buddy? She's your type!" Doug joked.

"Geez guys." I said, laughing. After a couple more hours of pub stuff, we all left at around eleven. It was a work day tomorrow and no one wanted to be late.

I walked outside and zippered up my coat. It was a cold summer night. I jumping into my 2008 Volvo and drove off into the night. I didn't have to drive far to get back to the apartment where I was staying.   I unlocked my room and walked in, clicking on the lights. A small kitchen to the right and a couch with a TV to the left, this was my home. I walked into the bedroom in the back and fell right into bed, and quickly fell asleep.

Chapter 2

I woke up the next day at seven AM, the exact time I should always wake up. A quick run to the kitchen and a quick bowl of Lucky Charms, and I was out. I jumped back into my Volvo and drove three miles to the local Best Buy. My blue uniform was a nice fit, and the nametag was an even better fit.

After a day of full boredom, I waited for the game on Saturday. Just one more day until pure awesomeness. I know how that sounds, but I'm in love with it. It's the best game in the world, and I was glad that I discovered it. On one windy October evening, I discovered the game that I loved.

On the walk back to my car (I had to park across the highway, which makes me take a walk under the highway through a tunnel), I stopped before going through the tunnel. On a dark and cloudy day like today, the tunnel was musty, and well, dark. I looked at my clock. Five on a cloudy afternoon and I could get hurt in there. It was pure cement, and I could see some water dripping from the top.

I took my pocket knife out of my pants pocket and placed it in my coat pocket for easy grabbing. If anything happened in here, I needed to be ready to defend myself. I slowly started to walk through. The only sound was my breathing, my footsteps, and the cars passing overhead. My heavy breathing was starting to overcome me. What, did I think I was going to be jumped? I was a couple of miles from the city. But still, anything could happen.

I kept my fingers closed around the pocket knife as I walked through the tunnel. One second it was silent, and then in another second a hand was on my shoulder and a raspy voice in my ear.

"Hey there little boy, want to have a fun time?" It said.

"Skup you!" I said, brushing the hand off my shoulder. In the dark light I could see a dark form of a man, most likely a hobo. He started to limp toward me.

"I don't want to hurt you…" he said, coughing. I started a quick jog through the tunnel. The end was so close; I was around halfway through it. But before I could make it someone grabbed me and pushed me to the right wall. My head crashed against the cement, filling my head with a headache. I struggled to get my pocket knife out.

"It's OK, I'm from the government!" the man tried to tell me. His breath was warm. I finally closed my fingers around my pocket knife and flicked open the biggest knife. Then I pulled it out of my pocket and into the man's hand holding me. From the little light inside I could see blood explode out of the wound. The man screamed and let go. Blood continued to spurt out as I shoved his hand away. Blood was leaking down his arm as I ran out of the tunnel.

When I ran into the sunlight I thought I was safe. But a man grabbed me from behind. I struggled, trying to kick my attacker. I saw the first man walk through the tunnel, holding his hand, blood spraying through his fingers.

"Crap." I said silently. The man held my hands behind me as the first walked up.

"You don't knife someone, mother skupper!" he yelled.

"You tell him!" the second said from behind me.

"You're skupping right, I'm not from the government. But I bet you a million dollars that these

23

fists can hurt as much as someone from the government!" the first yelled, and then punched me in the stomach. My air escaped me like it was being sucked out by a fan. I struggled for air as he punched me again. Then he punched me in the face once, twice, then three times. I felt warm blood in my mouth.

"Skup you!" The one behind me said. Then the unexpected happen. The druggy came out of the tunnel.

"Do you want a fun time?" he asked, and almost fell over.

"Who the hell is this?" the first one asked.

"I don't know. Who the skup are ya?" the second asked the man.

"My name's Obama!" the druggy said.

"What the hell?" the first asked.

"No, wait, it's Bill. Bill Clinton." The druggy said. If I could hit my hand to my forehead, I would. The two men laughed. They seemed to have forgotten about me. Then the first started to take something out of his pocket. Crap.

"Skup you man." The first said and shot two bullets into the druggy's head. Blood shot out from the back. I had to close my mouth to avoid throwing up. The druggy fell down hard on the pavement, and blood splattered onto the ground. Geez, this is getting to be too much. Who the skup were these guys? They owned guns, fought people they just met. Then it began to make sense.

I brought my elbow back into the second man's stomach, and heard him wheeze out air. Then I used this opportunity to jump up, then angle myself backwards. The second man slammed against the ground, with me on top of him. The man's hands automatically let go.

"Skup!" The first man said, and then brought up his gun. I quickly rolled off the unconscious man I was lying on and heard a gun fire. Blood splattered on the back of my shirt. He had accidentally shot the man that I had rolled off of. I refused to look behind me at the hole in the man's chest, so I ran to the bushes to the left. I heard the man fire one more bullet as I jumped behind the nearest bush.

It all made sense. The warm breath. The gun. His friend. His anger. Before I could take the proper precautions to prepare myself for what I might see I looked over the bush. The man had the gun pointed to his head. I couldn't take my eyes off as all the brain and blood contained in his head flowed out the opposite side that the gun was on. Then I started crying. I took the cell phone out of my pocket and dialed 911. Then I threw up.

A couple minutes later the police sirens were in the background as I cleaned my mouth up. When I wiped my sleeve across my face, I saw blood on it. Those skuppers really hit me hard. As the first officers came onto the scene, I just hoped that they would believe me. I was covered in blood, and there were three dead guys next to me. I wasn't in the best position. But somehow I knew that I would be believed. Because what I had found out was key.

His warm breath and crazy attitudes first let me know that he was drunk. I mean, no person just goes around looking for trouble and doesn't ask for anything like money. He just wanted to beat someone up. He must have had anger issues and the alcohol just made it worse.

His poor friend most likely just got sucked into this mess. A crazy man with a gun, I'd do anything for him too.

"Do you know who this man is?" One police officer asked me.

"No clue." I responded, covered in a blanket against the cold winds.

"Well he was just an average Joe, most likely got twisted up in some gang related stuff." The officer said.

"Did you check him for alcohol?" I asked. The officer looked at me strange.

"Now why would you infer that?" The police woman asked. I revealed too much. Now they thought I was involved.

"Cause that's when people act strange?" This was not good. I was blabbering on. Now they would think that I know something. I could tell it as the woman's eyes widened.

"I'm going to have to take you back to the station for further questioning." She said.

"I...I can't. I need to get home." I blabbered.

"I'm sure it can wait." She responded. Then she got up and started to talk to other policemen. I'm so screwed. If I run they will surely look into me and discover my secret. And I cannot have that happen. But if I stay with them, the same will happen. I was between a rock and a hard place. This could only end one way. And that way is them discovering my secret. But if I ran, then I would go on the 'Wanted' list. And that is way worse than just going into the station.

Ten minutes later I was riding in the backseat of a police car to the station. The ride there was pretty awkward; it was just me in the back and the driver up front. There was of course glass separating us, so I felt like a criminal. The driver did not attempt to talk to me during the trip; he just kept his eyes on the road and his cap on his head. When he finally parked and got out, he allowed me to let myself out. Then he walked behind me as I walked into the station. I guess he thought that I would try to escape or something. When I came to the front desk, the driver stepped in beside me and explained the situation to the secretary behind the desk.

"Just go sit down over there and we'll be with you shortly." The secretary said, pointing with his head over to where five metal chairs were positioned, with a short stack of magazines on a coffee table in front of the chairs. I slowly walked over to the chairs as my driver walked into an office on the other side of the large lobby.

I sat down in the middle chair and looked at the magazines. *Oprah Magazine*, no way I'm reading that. *Home Cooking*, not in a million years. *Entertainment Weekly* may be interesting. I picked it up and realized that it was dated two years ago. I set it back down. I guess I wouldn't be reading.

I took a look across the room I was in. It was connected to the lobby in a way that made it look like a hallway. A couple paintings of old men labeled the walls, most likely old police chiefs or something like that. Across from me was a clock with the police logo in front of the white backing. It was around six o'clock and outside it was starting to get dark. There was no music playing, just the typing of the secretary. I imagined that all he did all day was changing his Facebook status. *At work, bored. Still at work, a couple*

29

bad guys came in today. .Still at work... I laughed to myself.

Then I realized what a terrible situation I was in. I've been trying to cover up my secret for so long, and I haven't had a big problem like this since. I began thinking about what I would say if they discovered it. Would I go with the cliché 'I have no idea what you are talking about' or maybe 'It won't happen again'? And what if I say the wrong thing? I'm no Marty McFly -- I can't go back in time to change things. There is no "Back to the Future". And even if I could I would not go back and change what went on the day.

Again this was a time where my appearance did not help me. I had dyed hair, which might mean that I was looking for trouble. It's just a stereotype that people make of me. You see them try to avoid me on the street, even clerks watch me in stores. It's not like I have a skupping tattoo or earring, but people still look out for me. And not in a good way.

Also once they realize what I did, they will most likely attach my terribleness to this event, and somehow, some way attach me to this. I was not a part of this attack today, but they can always twist the story to make it like I was. Either way, this would not end well.

"Melvin?" A kind voice asked. I looked toward it. A man with a suit and tie was talking to me from an open door a couple of yards away.

"Yep." I said, standing up. The man motioned me into the room. I walked inside and noticed that this was an interrogation room. A bland metal table was there with metal chairs on both ends.

"Please have a seat." The man said. I sat down in a chair and the man sat down across from me.

"I didn't do anything…" I started.

"We don't know that yet. My name is Officer Jose, and this will go as fast as you want it to. Now why don't you start at the beginning?" The man said, and took a tape recorder out of his pocket, and placed it on the table before turning it on. I had no choice but to tell him. And if I lied then it would only make matters worse.

"Well at first I was walking home from work, and to get to my car I have to travel through this

31

tunnel. As I was about to walk through I realized how dark and dangerous the tunnel would be, and it was a cloudy day. So I got my pocket knife ready in my coat pocket if anything was to happen. As I started to walk through the tunnel I was approached by a homeless person who asked me if I 'wanted a good time'. I brushed him off and kept walking, trying to ignore him. Then I was assaulted by another man who pushed me into the wall of the tunnel and started saying that he was from the government and other crap that I didn't listen to. So I stabbed his hand to get him off of me."

"What? So you stabbed the man in the hand to get him off of you?" Jose asked.

"He wouldn't let go." I said, feeling foolish.

"You never asked him to 'Please get off'?" Jose said.

"I think it was implied." I shot back. I could see Jose making a mental note of this.

"Interesting. Please continue." He said, giving away nothing. I did not want him to get the wrong idea. So I continued my story.

"So after I stabbed him I started to run out of the tunnel. When I was out I got attacked by another man who held my hands behind my back. Then the first man came over,"

"The man who you stabbed?" Jose interrupted.

"Yes, the man I stabbed." I said.

"Carry on." Jose said back.

"The first man came over and punched me in the face and started swearing at me, saying how he was going to hurt me and such. He punched me a good ten times in the face, enough to make me bleed. Then the homeless man who I first saw came out of the tunnel. The man started talking nonsense to the man who was hurting me, saying how he was the President. So the man who I stabbed took out a black handgun and shot the homeless man in the head. I realized that I had to do something, so I landed on top of the man who was holding me and started to roll away when the man with the gun tried to shoot at me, and ended up shooting his partner. I dove behind some bushes and that's when he shot himself." I ended.

"And that's all?" Jose asked.

"Pretty much." I said.

"Now I heard that on the scene you asked one officer if they checked the man for alcohol. Why did you do this?"

"Well, because his breath was warm and he was acting crazy. I just connected the dots."

"We checked that man's body, and he was drunk." Jose frowned. I gave myself a little fist pump in my head. I knew it.

"Can I go now?" I asked, trying not to seem guilty of anything.

"Not yet. Now are you sure that you did not know any of the men in question?" Jose said.

"I did not know any of the men." I responded. Jose thought about this.

"Either another man or I will come back. You are instructed to not leave this room until told to." Jose said, turned off the tape recorder then walked out, closing the door behind him. I shrunk in my chair. Then a couple of minutes later another man walked in. This man had the same suit and tie that Jose had, but this man looked more serious. He sat down and placed a folder on the table, then looked up at me. He did not even say his name; he just went right into the details.

"When we were investigating your file we noticed something of interest." The man said. Oh, skup, he found it. This was the first time that someone has discovered it since it happened when I was twenty. This man, this aged man with carefully combed white hair and thin eyebrows, found it. I was forced into his trap.

"I know." I said, handing myself over.

"This changes the case dramatically." The man said, eyes peeking over reading glasses.

"I understand. But the two have no relation at all, believe me." I said.

"Unfortunately I cannot do that without hard evidence."

"Please sir..."

"But there is one option." My eyebrows rose.

"What?" I asked. The man got up and locked the door, then sat back down.

"I understand that you play ultimate frisbee on the team The Musers, is this correct?"

"Yes."

"We have reason to believe that someone on your team is holding a weapon that could endanger citizens of the Unites States of America. This man is now labeled as a terrorist." This man was serious.

"How do you know it is someone on my team?" I asked.

"We have an image of the man with your team uniform on." The man said, opened the file and spun the photograph around and pushed it over to the other side of the table. I picked it up, and looked at it. The picture was quite blurry and had a man, back to the photographer, wearing the uniform walking across the road. I could not even recognize who the man was, the picture was too blurry.

"I don't know who this is, but it looks like this man has the body of someone who would be on my team." I said, staring at the picture.

"Our sources say that this picture was taken after he acquired the weapon" The man opened up the folder again and took out a piece of paper with writing on it, then pushed it across the table to me. This paper had approximate heights and other dimensions of the man. This man could be anyone on my team -- Frank, John, Bill, Doug, even Fred.

"This could be anyone on my team." I said to the man.

"That's why we need you to figure out who it is. You help us with this, and I promise you, your secret will never get out." The man responded with his proposal.

"So this is blackmail?" I asked.

"Something like that." The man said.

"Is this even legal?" I said back, placing the papers on the table.

"You tell me." The man said and slid his card across the table. I read it, ROBERT E. BELLAMY, Director of the Federal Bureau of Investigation. Wow, the skupping FBI was getting into this. It must be pretty serious. Robert was right, it did not matter if it was legal or not, he was with the FBI, anything is legal to him.

"Wow, this is serious sir." I said, looking at Robert.

"Yes, yes it is. Now I need you to carry on with your life, and if you have *any* idea who this man may be, contact me on the number on the card. You can let yourself out." Robert said, then got up, grabbed the folder, and left the room. I sat there, scared out of my mind. This is skupped up. My world was now filled with blackmail, deception, and everything in between.

Chapter 3

As I got up and left the room, it seemed that everything was going in slow motion. My thoughts were pounding on my head. I quickly thought of everything that my team meant to me. What my *brothers* meant to me. They wouldn't do this. Robert must have it wrong. Maybe that man stole our uniform...impossible! I was not thinking straight.

I walked through the doors of the station and noticed my car waiting for me. They got it for me. I hopped into my Volvo and drove home. When I got into my apartment I laid down on the couch. I just needed to think about this. What the skup was I going to do? I had practice tomorrow, then a game on Saturday. Would I be able to think of who it might be by then? No, I'm going crazy. I know the people on my team. And none of them would ever hurt anyone.

But how well did I really know them. I mean I only see them usually three days a week, but is that enough? That is not even half of the week, how can I really know someone? I was being forced to define *know,* as if it was a new word that I just imagined. But these men, these men on my team, they are good men. Why would they even think about this? None of them had gotten in trouble with the police before. But then again, how do I really know these people? I don't live with them. I sometimes have lunch with them on days when we don't have practice, but other than that I never see them outside of ultimate.

Then the phone rang. The tone rang in my ears, begging me to get up. But I did not want to. I continued to lie on the couch. The phone continued to ring. After around seven rings it stopped and the caller recorded a voice message.

"Hello honey, this is your mother. I miss you, and I know that you are still recovering from your father's death, and I am too. But it has been two months now, and it's time we move on. I love you and please call me back." The message said, and then the phone went silent. I sat up, and then walked over to the phone.

"Message deleted." The phone said after I pressed the button.

"Move on, move on! You didn't give a crap that he died! Your selfish little skupper!" I screamed to the phone. Tears started to swell in my eyes. I sat back down on the couch, tears streaming down my cheeks. My parents divorced a while before my father died, and now my mother wanted back in. But she was the one that abandoned me all those years ago. And now *she* wants to get back? She needs to learn that I DON'T WANT APOLOGIES! I WANT YOU TO LEAVE ME ALONE!

As I screamed this in my head, the tears continued to come, down and down my cheek. I took a tissue and sneezed. My head hurt so much right now. I stood up and was about to go take a nap, before a letter slip under the door. I walked over and opened the door. No one was there. I opened the letter.

MELVIN,

I HOPE THAT YOU UNDERSTAND OUR ASSIGNMENT TO YOU. IF YOU ASSUME THAT YOU CAN GO AND NOT COMPLETE THIS, WE WILL FIND OUT. OUR SOURCES WILL BE WATCHING YOU, AND IF YOU DO NOT COMPLETE THE GIVEN ASSIGNMENT OR TELL ANYONE ABOUT IT YOUR SECRET WILL GO LIVE AND YOU WILL BE IMPRISONED.

Who the skup do they think I am? Who the *skup* do they think I am! I am not their pet, their animal. I do what *I* want to do, not what they want me to do. I'm fine with helping them out, but they don't trust me with it? What the hell do they think they are doing? They cannot control me. They *will not* control me. Screw them. This is my life. They could have taken that picture for all I skupping care. None of my friends would do this. None of them, and if I have to prove it I will.

After the encouraging yelling I did to myself, I walked into my room and took a nap. When I woke up and looked at the clock, my stomach was begging for food. I ignored the fact that the clock said ten o'clock PM; I reheated pizza from two nights ago. After that I fell back onto my bed and this time fell asleep for real. The next time I awoke it was time for work. I changed into my Best Buy uniform, clipped on my name tag, ate breakfast, and went outside to my car.

Inside my car I saw a note on the dashboard. *"Don't skup up."* It read in small type. I stood there with the note in my hands. The FBI made a copy of my car keys. Oh crap. I ripped the note in two then watched it drop to the ground. I slowly drove out of

Absolution Apartments and to Best Buy. When I went inside, my friend Darius greeted me.

"Letter for ya." He said, then walked away.

"Thanks?" I said, and then opened up the letter. *"Read our letters. They are not made for ripping."* Who the skup are these guys? I looked around me. No one was looking at me. These guys were messing with my mind. I can't let them win. I crumpled this letter and threw it into the trash.

I took my place at the front of the store to greet the customers. After a long day of helping old ladies find the best TV or teens find the best phone for texting, I finally exited the store and walked outside. The tunnel still had the yellow *Do Not Enter* tape surrounding it. I would have to take the long way, across the walking bridge a quarter mile down. When I got to the parking lot there was no note for me.

I drove back to my apartment and debated what I should do. After deleting another message from Mom I picked up the card that Robert gave me. I got out my laptop and looked up the FBI website. The first thing my eyes saw was Director: George Howard. My mouth dropped open. I clicked on his name and a

43

picture and bio greeted me. Before I could read the bio the familiar "Internet Explore cannot display the webpage". No doubt the FBI did this too. I tried refreshing the page with no luck.

"What the skup?" I said to myself. So this wasn't really the FBI that I was dealing with. But what was it really?

I looked at the card. From what I remember from my brief sight of the FBI homepage I remembered the address. The address on the card was the same. At least they tried to make it look a little legit. I looked at my clock on the wall. There was around two hours until practice. I had time.

I went back into my car and drove to the police station. The secretary glared at me from behind the desk.

"What do you want now Melvin?" he asked.

"I want to speak with Jose." I said.

"You know where to sit. I'll send him over." The secretary said, and then continued typing. I sat down in the same metal chair. I folded my hands across my lap, jittery with nervousness. Eventually Jose came out, with a different tie today.

"Come on." He said and walked into the same room. I sat down in the familiar chair across the table.

"You know the man that came in after you yesterday?" I asked.

"The secretary? He just told you that you could go..." Jose started.

"No! Robert Bellamy."

"Who?"

"The 'Director' of the FBI" I made the quotation marks in the air with my fingers.

"What are you talking about?" Jose asked. I explained everything Robert said to me, only excluding the blackmail and my secret.

"Hold on." Jose said and walked out of the room. He came back a couple of minutes later.

"What is it?" I asked.

"I reviewed the security tapes of this room." He said, and pointed to the camera behind him. It blended into the white background surprisingly well.

"Did you see him?" I said.

"I watched the entire footage. Why didn't you tell me about the blackmail?" he asked.

"I dunno." I responded.

"Well has this man contacted you at all since yesterday?" Jose asked.

"I found notes in my car and at work." I said, and explained what the notes said. Jose nodded, and then looked at his watch.

"I don't have time for this today; can we meet at the same time tomorrow?" Jose asked.

"Of course," I said, standing up.

"And if you get another note, this time don't rip it up please." Jose added. I tried not to smile.

"Yes sir." I said, and we both walked out. When I got back to the apartment, I got my cleats and changed for ultimate, checked the schedule to see what field we were practicing at today, then drove over to it.

After a good ten minute drive I came to Pioneer High School. I drove around back to the fields behind it, and saw everyone stretching. I walked out and joined them. After the usual small talk (I left out what happened in the tunnel and the FBI stuff) we got a couple discs out and started throwing them to our partners. We knew the drill. Twenty minutes of throwing, ten of that used for backhands, the other ten for forehands.

As I ran to the other side of the field John threw me the first backhand. I caught it with one hand and sent one right back at him. John was a nice guy, but could he be the terrorist? What was I thinking? Robert Bellamy doesn't exist...so the information he gave me must not exist either...right? I pondered this as John and I exchanged the disc back and forth. Then Frank screamed out "Switch!" I changed to forehand.

I flicked one to John and watched him do the same to me. None of these men would hurt anyone, right? I have to get this idea out of my head. Robert Bellamy does not exist. He does not exist... Does not exist... Does not exist... Does not exist. Or maybe he does. Maybe the website just had the information wrong. Maybe George Howard was, I don't know, CFO and I just read it wrong. But a little voice in my head told me I was right. How did I get sucked into this? And how the skup can I get out?

"OK guys bring it in!" Frank called out. We joined in a circle. This was perfect. A chance to just play a short game to three, a chance to just play some ultimate and forget the world, leave it behind. As we split the teams, my team had to wear yellow pennies over our Musers uniform.

"The force will be woods," Bill told us as we walked over to our side of the field. The other team pulled the disc and we ran toward each other. Bill picked up the disc and right away threw it to me. I caught it and scanned the field for someone to be open. My defender was on stall six.

"Get open!" I screamed. I saw Luke make a cut, and I flicked a forehand to him. He just barely caught it one-handed, and then threw a quick backhand to Bill. Once Bill nodded his head, I knew what to do. I started sprinting to the end zone, catching my defender off guard. As I made it inside the end zone, I could see the shadow of the disc making its way toward me.

"Up!" Several random men shouted. This meant that the disc was in the air. I saw that the disc was making its way down to a flutter as my defender caught up to me. When the disc started to float down, I faked a jump. My defender jump up, trying to defend me, but was met with air. The disc slowly floated into my open hands. One-zero.

A couple of minutes later when I threw the pull, I remembered what went on during the past couple days. The FBI. Jose and Robert. I tried to move on by remembering the saying *"You may stop, but the game doesn't"*. I tried to push the memories out of my head, and plug them in with ultimate. But when the man I was covering caught the point, and I was halfway across the field, I knew it would be tough.

"What's wrong?" Luke asked once we were on our sides.

"Nothing." I lied.

"Come on Melvin. You can tell us." Bill said. I considered it.

"I got jumped yesterday in the tunnel next to Best Buy." I said. Technically it wasn't a lie. I watched my team gasp.

"Are you OK?" Luke asked.

"Ya, I'm fine, it just doesn't put the best memories in your head." I responded. The team nodded.

"Well if you want a water break, just let us know." Bill said as the other team pulled the disc.

"Sure," I said, and started running to the other team. I caught the disc and threw it to Mark. Mark quickly flicked it to Fred. Fred gave it a big backhand to Bill in the end zone. The disc was smacked down by the other team. I don't know what was going through the man's head when he threw it to the end zone, but it was smacked down by me before he had a chance rethink it. I bombed it back to Bill, and this time he pushed aside his defender and caught it in the end zone. Two-one. Let's finish this.

The hot summer sun was visible in the cloudless sky as we played. Countless turnovers were viewed, as the other team did not give up easily. So we kicked it up. Extra fakes and countless cuts were made as we tried to distract and disable the other team. One time poor Luke threw a low one to Mark (the defenders were tough) and Mark had to layout (dive) for it. He got it and jumped up almost exactly after and flicked it to Bill. Bill then nodded again, and I sprinted to the end zone. He bombed a backhand and I made a layout catch.

After the game we had some more small talk.

"So how's the wife, Frank?" Bill asked.

"She left me. Cheating with another man." The whole team gasped.

"Are you going to file for a divorce?" Someone asked.

"What else would I do? Continue to let her skup around behind my back?" Frank asked.

"You have a point there." Someone said.

"But it is quite sad. I really liked Betsy." Frank said, sadness in his eyes.

"Speaking of really liking," Doug said, turning to me.

"Ya Melvin, did you ask Gloria out yet?" Mark said.

"I don't go to Exo-Politics every night like you fool. I have a life!" I laughed, and the team joined in.

"Staying in the pub until eleven every night is a life…sort of." Doug said, laughing.

"Maybe after the next game, if we win." I said.

"But if we didn't win, you could get the guilt factor." Bill said, making a point.

"I can picture it now…'Gloria, I feel very sad after what went on today, us losing and everything, and it would make my life if you would be my girlfriend.' Perfect moment!" Doug mocked.

"Ah, Shut up." I responded, laughing.

"Hey, did you ever fix up your basement, Mark?" Frank asked. Then the small talk continued. Then I realized that us guys, we had problems like everyone else. But we had a way to deal with it.

Playing ultimate frisbee and talk about it. I know that I couldn't tell them about what has been going on, I just can't. I would hate for them to be sucked into it with me.

When I left after ten minutes of talking I got into my Volvo and drove back home. I wonder if Robert Bellamy would be angry at me for telling Jose about him. Only one way to find out. I did not really think about who could be the terrorist in my group, I could not even try to imagine. I cannot imagine a world where someone on my team could even try to kill people. They had problems and lives already. I couldn't picture Mark or Frank having a nuclear missile in their basement. I laughed at the thought.

Chapter 4

The next day when I opened my car, I saw another note. *"Don't bother driving to work today. Call it your punishment for telling Jose."* This cannot be good. What would be waiting for me at work? Every red light I got stopped at I wanted to speed through just to see what was at work. I was like a skupping little boy on Christmas Eve.

As I walked through the doors and started my shift, nothing went on at first. Then Darius walked up to me and said that the boss wanted to see me. I said thanks, and then walked to the boss's office.

"Hello, Melvin." The boss said, glaring at me.

"Hello? What can I do for you sir?" I asked.

"I'm firing you." The man said, giving away nothing in his eyes.

"What? Why?" I said, surprised.

"I heard from a source that you've been giving customers up to fifty percent off the price of select items."

"What? I would never do that!" I tried to say.

"Don't make this worse." My boss said.

"Was the source Robert Bellamy, huh!" I yelled.

"He asked not to reveal his name." he said.

"You've got to be skupping kidding me!" I said.

"Melvin, get out." His voice was stern.

"Did he tell you he was from the FBI too!" I yelled.

"I will call the police." That shut me up. I don't want to go to the office, then straight to Jose; he'll think that I'm crazy. Just another crazy man who gets in trouble because of problems in the head. But that was not me.

"Yes, sir." I said, and was about to exit the office.

"Oh, and Melvin!" My boss said.

"Yes?" I asked.

"Give your uniform and name tag to Darius tomorrow."

"Yes sir." I said sadly.

I walked back to my car (tunnel still having CSI working there) and was expecting a note. No luck. I had put the other note in the glove department. I checked, and it was still there. As I drove home I tried to look for a store with a *Now Hiring* sign on it, but I knew that it would be useless. With this economy I would never get another job. The Best Buy job just gave me enough to survive. Now I had no idea what to do. I felt like I was being pushed over the edge.

As I looked in the rearview mirror I saw tears start to race down my cheek. I also cry when I'm sad. I guess it makes me feel better. As I walked into apartment room number eleven I sat down on my couch and turned on the TV. I watched the news for a bit then remembered my meeting with Jose. I wonder how this will go...

I grabbed the keys off of the kitchen counter and walked into the parking lot to my car. Another note was waiting for me. "*Don't screw up again, buddy*." I stuffed the note into the glove compartment with the other and drove to the station.

"May I see the notes?" Jose asked once we were inside the familiar room.

"Yep." I said and tried to get them out of my pocket. I laid them out on the table and Jose picked them up. I saw him look them over.

"You're lucky these aren't ransom letters." He laughed at his own joke. I stared.

"This is serious." I said.

"Just trying to make a joke, geez." Jose said.

"It's fine."

"So these started appearing when?" Jose asked.

"Right after I met Robert."

"Robert Bellamy?"

"Right. I thought that they would stop after I told you, but they continued." I said.

"OK, well first we'll scan them for fingerprints, tell all police in the area to look for this Robert guy." Jose said.

"Thanks." I said.

"You were smart coming to us." Jose said.

"I know." I said, knowing all of this. It's always the same, what they say. Thanks this, thanks that, but even then it's all script.

"Do you want to go upstairs as I scan the prints?" Jose asked.

"Sure, I've got nothing else better to do." I said as I followed Jose out the door and to a set of stairs. We silently climbed up, and came to a door on the left. I walked through and came into a big room with giant windows lining the left wall. On the walls were countless books on wood bookcases.

"Sir, this doesn't look like a place where we would scan for prints," I started, but Jose interrupted.

"Listen, Melvin. I brought you up here because downstairs is too dangerous a place for me to reveal this information to you." Jose said quickly, looking around the room to see if anyone was listening.

"What's so bad about the information?" I asked.

"This Robert guy, I've heard of him before." Jose said.

"When?"

"He said that he was a member of the FBI and asked to see some classified folders. We asked to see a badge, and he couldn't get one out. So we told him we cannot reveal those folders unless he shows a badge. So he said that he'll come back the next day and show us his badge. But he never returned."

"Did he look the same as he does now?" I asked.

"It was a couple of years ago, so he looked a bit younger. But nevertheless, we recorded his arrival, and now his name has come up yet again." As Jose spoke, neither he nor I were aware that his head was now in the middle of a sniper's scope. The sniper slowly put his finger around the trigger. He would not miss this shot.

"So what do you think I should do?" I asked, now concerned.

"Well first, I believe we should….," Before Jose could finish, a blackish-red substance exploded out of the right side of his head. It took me only a second to realize that he had been shot. As his lifeless body lay on the ground, I figured I was next. So as the carpet that I was standing on started to fill with blood, I ran to the door. The farther I was from the window, the better.

I tried the handle. The door was locked, and I could not get out. Then the door flew open and a man with a mask burst into the room, knife in hand.

"SKUP!" I screamed as the man ran toward me. I quickly flung myself to the left, avoiding his attempt to stab me. He flung himself at me yet again, and this time I grabbed his hand. He used all his strength to propel the knife into my head, but I pushed him back.

I started running to the desk that was shoved in the corner. The man tackled me and we both landed behind the desk. Again the man tried to stab me, and I tilted my head to avoid the knife, and the knife dug into the carpet. As the man tried to get it out, I kicked his stomach, which caused him to step backwards.

Then my mind started to think of a plan. The sniper that had killed Jose was probably looking to shoot me. If he saw my knife-wielding friend, he could accidently shoot him instead. So if I got the man close enough to the windows so the sniper could see him, bang! No more annoying knife-guy.

I grabbed both of the man's arms as he ran at me from across the room, and pushed him forward. He stumbled to the windows, then stopped himself, and started running to me again. I realized that my plan would not work, because the sniper most likely knew what his partner did and did not look like.

The man swung his knife at me, and I ducked, but not fast enough. The knife skimmed my arm, causing minimal bleeding. Since I was this low, I threw myself forward and took the man down. As we both hit the ground, I struggled to get the knife out of the man's hands.

The sniper looked through the scope and realized that he couldn't get a clean shot at me. The shot would either hit his partner, or miss completely. He decided to wait out until a better shot approached.

As I rolled off of the man, he stuck out his fist and punched me where the knife had skinned me. I screamed in pain as the man attempted to stab me yet again. I picked up a chair from in front of the desk and flipped it so that the legs were facing my attacker. My attacker forced a confused look to his face.

I started sprinting toward the man, and the legs of the chair caught him. I continued pushing until we came to the big windows, then I brought my head down so the sniper could not see me. But I continued pushing, and when we came right before the window I pushed with all my might.

The sniper saw what I was doing. I was pushing my attacker to the windows, hoping to push him through. And I had ducked low so I couldn't be seen. "Smart punk", the sniper thought.

I continued to push and when we reached the windows I gave it one final push. The man and the chair legs smashed through the window. I stopped and let go of the chair. The man fell with the chair and the shards of glass four stories to the ground. I heard a smash and breaking of glass as they hit a car below.

I quickly ran from the window, because the sniper could see me. I ran to the door and pushed it open. Then I ran downstairs. My plan was to get into my car and away before the sniper could get out of the building he was in.

I ran through the lobby, no one asking questions. I sprinted out the doors, and into my Volvo. When I got inside my car I realized that I had left the case folder inside of the room. I'll have to get it later, I told myself as I quickly drove away. Those folders were quite important, and I needed to get them later. Then I looked in the rearview mirror and realized I had bigger problems on my hands.

A black truck was behind me, and looking through the front of the car, I saw a man with a bandit mask in the front seat, driving. This must be the sniper. I turned the wheel to the right and took the first exit. From there I weaved in and out of back roads, trying to lose this man. I didn't care about getting lost; I could find my way back later.

As I continually looked in the rearview mirror, I saw that this man was not giving up. But as I turned my eyes back to the road, I saw that I had turned onto a dead end road. As I approached the wall of trees before me, I spun the wheel to the left and felt my car spin with it. I saw the confusion in the man's face behind me as I spun. When I was facing the right direction, I pushed down on the petal.

I sped past the car and saw in the rearview mirror as the man turned his car around, now far behind me. As I sped past him, I started thinking about which way I would turn. I would go right, and then just keep driving. Hopefully I would lose him by then. After driving away, I realized that I had done it. After a quick fist pump to myself, I drove to where I thought the highway was. I had to get home. Tomorrow was the big game, so I needed a good night's rest. I looked at the clock in my car. It was almost six. I had enough time. But what would I have for dinner?

As these thoughts went through my head, I did not notice the green Hybrid following me. And when I finally did, I dismissed it was being just another car.

I drove right onto the highway, and noticed that the Hybrid was still behind me. In the same lane. Going the same way. I started to get suspicious. So I sped up, I saw the Hybrid do the same. I slowed down to see if I could see a bandit hat, with no luck. So what? The guy most likely took it off. I quickly changed lanes, then at the last second, changed back. It ended just as I hoped, another car would go into the spot that the Hybrid was in only seconds before, and now that I moved back, the Hybrid had no space to move back to.

I took my exit off of the highway and onto my exit, then onto the main road. As I drove into the parking lot of the apartments where I was staying, I looked in the rearview to see if there were any green cars around. And there were none. I was safe, for now.

I got out of the car, locked it, and went inside the complex to my apartment. There was a note waiting for me. *"Enjoy seeing a dead Jose?"* the note said. I screamed and threw the note. It, being made out of paper, slowly floated to the ground. I check my messages. Just one from Mom, and it was deleted before it was even listened to.

There was nothing on the TV that wasn't boring, so I just watched the news. There was nothing about Jose or the shootings, but I knew that it would be on the news shortly. So I just watched how a skupping priest did that to a child and how a robber did this to a house. Boring.

I continued to watch for around an hour, before making my dinner. Good old "Mac and Cheese" always fills me up after a long day of being fired and seeing someone get sniped. But the memories sent me to the bathroom, and soon I was throwing up in the sink.

After some more TV I slowly drifted to bed. But when I was sleeping I did not notice the change of scenery, or even when I woke up once in the middle of the night to a pitch dark room. But even then I was too sleepy to notice the change. I slowly went back to sleep.

Chapter 5

But then the white lights started to get inside my eyelids, so I woke up. When I did at first, I did not notice the change. Then I started to see the bars and the tight space. I opened my eyes to the fullest. It took about ten seconds for my eyes to adjust. Then another ten to inspect myself to see if I was hurt. My shirt was gone, and I was wearing jeans. Someone had changed my clothes.

I inspected where I was. It seemed that I was in some sort of dog cage, around two feet wide and five feet long. The bottom was all plastic, and the bars felt like metal. Why was I in here? Who the skup had put me in here?

I looked past the cage. I was in a white room. A single door painted white was to my right. To my left was nothing but white walls.

"Hello?" I said, quietly at first. No response. Not like I was expecting one anyway. This is just like in the movies. I screamed again, just to see if someone would come to get me. I usually wake up at around seven, so it should be around that time. There were no windows or anything of that sort, so I couldn't see outside.

My stomach rumbled. I wanted breakfast, and I doubt I would get it here. Whoever took me was most likely taking me for hostage, which meant no food. But who would take me hostage? My mom? The ultimate guys? It didn't make any sense.

After yelling for someone to come and give me food (I said skup a lot), I sat down, my head barely touched the top of the cage, even though I was sitting and crouched. The cage was around two or three feet high, which was one small dog cage.

My stomach rumbled some more. I thought that a human can survive for around three days without food, but I did not know if that was true. I was starving, and I've never done a fast or anything like that, so this was extremely hard. I know that I just need to think of something else.

I bet the men who tried to kidnap me in Exo-Politics had something to do with this -- them or the sniper. Or maybe they are working together. But why would they want me? What have I ever done to them?

Is it punishment for driving away from the sniper? It was kind of common sense! I thought of the first question that all police ask: do you have any enemies? I thought this through.

Maybe it was some people from a rival ultimate frisbee team. Maybe Robert Bellamy is from The Cats or even maybe The Space Ducks. But would they seriously snipe my friend, kidnap me, and starve me inside a dog cage? That seems a little much for just losing a game. What is going on!

Unfortunately I do not wear a watch, so I had no idea what time it was. I estimated that it was around ten or eleven, I had spent tons of time in this cage and it was starting to show. I was not cold, and considering the fact that I did not have a shirt, there had to be some sort of heating system in this room. Nice of my terrorist friends to give me some sort of comfort. But why take off my shirt? And why put jeans on me? It made no sense.

My stomach continued to growl. Why me and why this? Why the skup would anyone want to capture me? I know that it was clichéd, that the main character did not know why he/she was captured, and then at the end they remember some big secret that reveals everything. But that is not me, and this is not that situation.

My secret has nothing really to do with anything. And it is not just my secret, it was Ryan's too, but now he's dead, killed two months after the dreaded rainy day that pretty much ruined my life. It was horrible what happened, so that's why I was so distressed about Robert saying that he knew.

But what if he didn't? What if he was lying? He never told me my secret, so why should I think that he knows? But if that is true, how did he know that I had a secret in the first place? Maybe he just said that to make me do what he wanted me to do. Everyone has a secret, right? So in that case all that he had to do was say something about a secret and I would automatically freak out, right?

As I was thinking of this my stomach rumbled again. I screamed for someone to get me food. No one answer, as I expected.

This is crazy. Why would someone kidnap me? WHY ME? I did not do anything to anyone. It was Ryan that did it, not me. So why the skup am I being held here, and being starved to death?

Just then the door flew open. Two men wearing bandit masks walked in, all in black. One of them took something out of his pocket, a taser. I started to squirm inside the cage. I quickly looked for a way out. I rattled the bars and scurried around. Then when I was rattling the bars on the backside of the cage, a sharp pain flew into my back.

I screamed, and it felt like fire exploding out of my mouth. This was worse than a licking a battery, over shocking yourself. I fell to the bottom of the cage, shaking and rolling. I couldn't control my movements. I felt myself moving, and I saw the cage wiggle around. I was shaking and I couldn't do anything to stop it. I tried to stop, but I just couldn't. My vision started to get more and shakier. Soon it was getting to be too much. I tried to close my eyes, but I had no control.

I could feel the eyes on my back. They were most likely laughing at me. Eventually I stopped wiggling and started to settle. Although I couldn't move, I heard one of the men open the cage door and grab my legs. He then dragged me out. When my

71

entire body was out of the cage, he grabbed me by the arms and his partner took my feet. Together they brought me through countless hallways, painted white like the room. I tried to move, but I was paralyzed.

Soon we came to a door, and inside was a white table like the white walls. They laid me down on the table. I tried to use this opportunity to roll off, and skup these jerks. But I couldn't move. But I could talk.

"What the hell did I do to you? Let me skupping go!" I screamed at them. And they stared back at me.

"Sadly, we cannot do that. Now we need some information from you, and if the only way to make you tell us is torture, let it be." The man on the left said.

"You can't skupping do this! Skup you! I'm not telling you anything!" I screamed at them.

"We need to know whose frisbee is always brought to your ultimate games." The one on the right said.

"What the skup? Why the hell does that matter!" I yelled.

"Just answer the question!" The left yelled. This was nuts. Why did they want to know who brought the disc? Why did it matter? Now I have a way of life that I live, and that way tells me that whatever these jerks want to know, I won't tell them. If they think that they can just kidnap me, starve me, and do all this other crap to me, and I'll tell them my secret? No skupping way.

"We'll give you twenty seconds to tell us. After that, you will scream." The one on the right said quietly.

"Listen to my words. Skup you!" I screamed. The man on the left started to count down from twenty. I continued to lie (what else could I do? It was not a taser that hit me, but some sort of disabling device) down on the table, waiting. After twenty seconds, the man on the left spoke.

"I'm very sorry for this." He said.

"Do your skupping worse." I said.

"As you wish." The man on the right said, and took a monkey wrench out of his pocket. Then he walked over and set both ends on my nose. This was gonna really hurt.

He slowly started to twist. I felt the cold metal bars on both sides hit both sides of my nose. Then they started digging in. I kept my head high. Then it broke skin. The cold was briefly interrupted by warm blood. I felt each single stream race down my cheek, down my neck, and down my chest. The exact same was happening on the other side of my face.

I squinted my eyes. Both men were silent, watching, as the man on the right slowly squeezed the wrench. Then I heard the crack. My nose was broken. I felt a rush of blood explode out of my nose.

"AHHHHHHHHHHHHHHHHH!!!!!!! SKUP YOU!!!!!!!" I screamed. But the man continued to squeeze. The man on the left smiled. The two bars of cold metal kept slowly going toward each other. I felt pieces of skin get mixed in with the blood as the wrench tightened. More bones were breaking in my nose, one after the other.

The feeling of pure hunger was forgotten as the two sides raced toward each other. I continued to scream.

"WHY THE SKUP DOES IT MATTER TO YOU! IT'S JUST A BLASTED DISC!!!!!!" I yelled. The men ignored me. Skup them, I didn't even know who brought the disc. It was always there when I arrived. But this thought was quickly pushed out of my head as the two sides of the wrench were pushed in.

More bones continued to break. Eventually the two ends will meet each other, right? Then they'll stop, right? But this was not very far away. I screamed as I felt both ends of the wrench touch. The man stopped screwing them in and stepped back, allowing the wrench to hang. I screamed and screamed some more.

"Tell us, or the wrench will be the least of your problems." One man said. I did not know who because my vision was blurred from the tears in my eyes. The blood was seeping into my mouth, giving me the warm taste of iron. It was also sliding down my chest, making it look like I was in a bloody fight. I was.

"Skup you! I'll like to see you do this to me when I'm not paralyzed! You sick cowards! You mother skuppers! I'd skup you up so bad you wouldn't know what skupping hit you!" I yelled.

"And that's why we keep you down." One man said, laughing.

"You think this is a joke! You sick piece of crap! Skup you! Where's your leader? That sick coward! He's making you do all the torturing while he watches from behind a curtain? SKUP HIM! SKUP YOU!" I continued to yell, blood mixing in with the spit in my mouth. I started to choke, so I spat out a big wet chunk of blood at my captors.

They laughed and one man left the room for one quick moment and came back with a washcloth and a bucket of water.

"Oh, crap! NO! NO SKUPPING WAY! NO!" I screamed, fearing for my life.

"Ah, shut the hell up." The man with the washcloth said, and placed it over my mouth. Then the man with the water walked over. I continued to yell at my captors through the washcloth, my sound muffled. Then the man poured the water through the cloth. I felt it storm down my throat, and I struggled to breathe.

But each time I tried to take a breath, water would seep through. The man just continued to pour it right down my throat. My coughing was now so loud it I could no longer beg them to stop. It was just a blasted disc! Why did they have to skupping water board me for it!

I choked on the water that seemed to continually flow down my mouth, I struggled to breathe, to even swallow it. I would spit out water, and it would come right back down on me. The hell with gravity!

When the man finished with that pail of water, he walked back outside and came back with another one. But when he was walking back in, I felt a finger move. I was slowly regaining my movement. And then all of a sudden, I knew that I could move. So when the man was close enough, I flung out my leg and hit the pail. The water flew up and smacked him in the face. The man fell to the ground. I struck out my right arm and wacked the other man. He let go of the washcloth in surprise, and I sat up on the table. I yanked the wrench from my nose, blood pouring, and struck the man in the head with it. Blood erupted up like a volcano.

As I jumped off of the table, the first man was getting up. I swung the wrench like a baseball bat and smacked the man in the nose. Blood spurted out like what happened to mine. The man fell to the ground, in pain. I walked above him and dropped the wrench. It landed on his face and the blood that was on his nose suddenly leapt into the air. The second man was on the ground, not breathing.

"Mess with me will ya?" I yelled.

I ran out of the room, covered in blood. My chest and entire body was covered in blood, just to add to my troubles. As I ran through the hallway the scene was like a nurse's outfit, white but with a little red in the center. Where the hell was I?

I started to run, trying to figure this place out. They wanted to confuse me, and it was so working. All the doors and walls seemed the same. They were the same. It made no sense whatsoever.

Then the hallway took a sharp right turn and I came to a door with a bright red EXIT sign above it. I pushed it open and alarms went off all around me, the annoying fire alarm type of sound.

"Skup." I said as I ran through the door, and outside was a line of metal steps leading down to the pavement. I ran down them, and felt the chill of having no shirt on. It was like running outside to an abandoned parking lot, there was just pavement and no cars. But as I looked forward I saw a green car all the way in the back left corner. I sprinted to it, and having rocks ripping into my bare feet was not as bad as having my nose practically ripped off.

I tried the door, it was open, and so I jumped into the front seat. There was a blue shirt in the right seat with the Muse logo on it. I was meant to find this car. I wonder if I would drive away and someone would either snipe me or kill me in some other way. There's only one way to find out. I reached over the wheel and grabbed a set of keys that were laying there.

I shoved the keys into the ignition and started up the car. Then I punched the petal with my foot, and the car surged forward. I sped past trees and other bushes before coming to a fence, opened. I sped right through. I followed signs until I came to a highway. This all looked very familiar. I must be relatively close to home.

After driving for a good ten miles I past a sign that advertised my exit to Absolution Apartments. Then when I looked ahead, I saw a very familiar Volvo. As I drove a bit closer, and looking at the license plate, I realized it was mine. I couldn't see who was driving, but I knew that the someone who had stolen it was now driving my Volvo. It was most likely one of the men who captured me. As I drove forward a bit, the person who was driving my car seemed to notice me. He or she started to weave in and out of traffic.

The man quickly changed lanes. I tried to change with him, but he quickly changed back. When I tried to move back another car had taken my place. There was no way I could continue to follow him. When I get back I'll just call the police and report my car being stolen. I'll just "forget" the fact that I swiped a car too.

When I took my exit and stopped for a red light I saw my car in two lanes over. The man must be going to loot my apartment. Not on my watch. I followed the man to the apartment building. When he parked, I did the same across the lot. I sat in the car and watched as the man got out of his car. Then my head started to hurt as my mouth formed an O.

The man who got out of the car, and took out the familiar keys out of his pocket, was me. It was I, in the exact same clothes that I wore the day that I drove home from the sniping of Jose. I ran to the back of the car as myself walking into the building. The car was a Hybrid. A green Hybrid.

"What the skup." I said, my mouth in a perfect O. It was me that chased me yesterday in the green Hybrid. But if I'm me, then who was that who was me now? Some type of clone? But I knew deep down in my heart that it was me. That is the way that I drive, the way that I walk, even the way that I get things out of my pockets.

Was this some sort of weird time-travel deal? Could my captors have somehow made me travel back in time? Then I heard a faint ringing in the backseat of the car. I opened the door, and found a Verizon TIRO phone. It was ringing. I opened it and put it to my ear.

"I suppose that you've seen yourself by now." A raspy voice said on the other end.

"What is going on?" I screamed into the phone.

"Nothing that you would ever understand." The voice responded.

"Let me be! What did I ever skupping do to you?" I said.

"You have two choices: One, you meet yourself and blow this whole operation. Two, you walk over to the HAARP Cemetery down the street and go to the top of the hill." The voice said.

"What the skup is this operation! Why me!" I yelled.

"You have your choices. If we don't see you at the Cemetery in three hours we'll start killing all the ones that you love, starting with your mother and ending with Frank." Then the voice hung up. I realized that this was not my choice. These men most likely had others that they want to hurt...and I did not want to be the one to encourage that. Also if I went to the cemetery I could find out what is going on. So I guess the cemetery it is. But first I would have to get ready.

I drove over to the nearest gun store I could find, and when I went inside I automatically felt like a fish out of water. Shotguns and other brands lined the shelves. This was a place for people with deerskin vests and cowboy hats, not me. But I had to protect myself.

I walked over to the desk where a man with a big mustache and an ever bigger stomach waited for me.

"Hi I'm looking for a handgun." I said plain and simple.

"What kind." The man said, not moving.

"Something that's easy to shoot, that will kill quickly, and that inexperienced people like me will be able to use." I said, the words coming out of my mouth like bullets.

"The back wall over there will have what you need. Any one of them." The man said.

"Thanks." I said and walked over to the wall. All the guns looked around the same, so I guess that what I was looking for was just color and style. And even that did not really matter that much. I just need a gun to use if things got out of hand at the cemetery, not to show off to my animal killing friends.

I picked one off the shelf that looked decent. It was all black, with a simple trigger and handle. I looked at the price. One hundred and fifty dollars. Came with twenty free rounds. I reached into my pocket for my wallet, and then remembered that my "other" most likely had my wallet and my money. I felt around to make sure, and I was right.

I peeked behind me. The man was texting behind the desk, eyes glued to the screen. I slowly took the gun off of the wall. I know that either way if I walk outside with this gun some sort of alarm activator on the gun will alert the man behind the desk and alarms will go off. But I'll be going to a cemetery. Who the skup looks for a robber in the cemetery?

I turned to the glass doors, gun in my pocket. I quickly turned to the staff member again. I was clear for another ten seconds. So I ran. The man automatically looked up as my feet made loud noises as I spirited through the store.

"What the skup are you doing?" he yelled after me.

I ran through the doors and into my car. I heard loud alarms rage on inside the store. The man grabbed his phone to call the police. I backed up, put the gun in the passenger seat, and started to drive away. Moving away, I put the store in my rearview mirror.

Before I could hear sirens in the distance, I slowly pulled into HAARP Cemetery, the rustic metal sign blowing in the wind. I drove up to the hill and parked. I put the gun into my inside coat pocket and slowly walked up to the top of the hill. My spine was chilled as I walked past various tombstones. The sky was blocked by grey clouds, giving the world a dark tone.

As I approached the top of the hill, I could not see anyone. I checked to make sure the gun was still there, and continued walking. When I got to the top I looked over the cemetery. The clouds blocked out every single ray of light that would ever want to burst through to the earth. I looked over, and felt like the ruler of this cemetery, the ruler of all the cluttered tombs and dead bodies.

All light was gone. My life felt chilled, I could feel my soul turn to ice. What the skup has my life turned into? This weird time travel crap was messing up my life. I felt my nose. Most of the blood was gone, and I knew that it would take a while for my nose to heal. The pain bugged me like an annoying talkative skupper in school. But I would learn to ignore it. But for now this cemetery was mine, and I was a god of a shrinking universe.

"Melvin?" A voice asked behind me. I turned around. An old man was standing there, bushy white eyebrows and wrinkles from lack of sleep. He was wearing a black coat, black hat, and black pants.

"What the heck do you want?" I asked.

"You do not know how important you are to this operation." He said, frowning.

"What operation? What the skup is going on!" I yelled.

"Take my hand." He said and held his hand out.

"Why the hell would I take your hand?" I asked.

"Currently you are in your reality. You need to come to mine for me to tell you anything else." I grabbed his hand. Instantly the scene changed. I was still at the top of the cemetery, but it was night. The only light came from the moon, which lit the tombs within their dark setting. Leaves blew all around, and the trees were collapsed on the ground.

"Are you for real?" I asked.

"What is real? What is reality?" the man asked, still frowning.

"How the heck am I supposed to know? All of you think that I know skupping everything! But here's a news flash: I don't!" I screamed.

"But you do know." He said.

"How the skup am I suppose to know what you think I do! Who would teach me!?" I yelled.

"You learned, Melvin. And you would have continued to learn if you had only stayed at the white room,"

"What! To continue being tortured? No skupping way! You can't control me! Why me!"

"You are more important then you think."

"How the hell so!"

"I cannot explain now,"

"Ya that's what they all skupping say!"

"We have reasons."

"Oh shut up! Reasons! You think that can save you! I don't know who the hell you are or why you're here, but I can beat the crap out of you any day!"

"But that wouldn't be a smart choice,"

"What, are you going to send me back in time again? Or turn me into a skupping newt!"

"I am not something of the supernatural, but the super-powerful."

"What is that suppose to mean!"

"I am more powerful then you realize."

"Skup you!"

"Is that your final answer?"

"I don't answer to you or anyone! To hell with you all!"

"Then I'm sorry about this." The man took a step to me.

"You skupping touch me, I'll put a bullet in your chest." I said, taking out my gun and pointing it at the man's chest.

"You fire that at me, you will regret it." He said, his voice raising.

"I'm the only one that can make threats here!" I yelled, aiming the gun.

"Don't even think about it." The man's voice was now as fierce as the cold wind that brushed me. Then he opened his mouth, revealing thousands of jagged teeth. He let out a screech that broke out into my ears like a raging infection.

Chapter 6

I aimed and pulled the trigger. The man's chest exploded with blood. As he fell, I started to run. I did not notice the man starting to get up behind me. Half of his lung was hanging out of his open hole in his chest, but he walked toward me. The teeth were revealed, and the eyes were a dark brownish-red, and his bushy eyebrows were now gone. I turned around.

"What the skup!" I yelled and shot his chest again. He let out another screech as his hanging lung exploded, sending blood all over the frozen grass. I sent another two bullets into the man's chest. He screeched while walking toward me. Then his walk turned into a run. So I ran too.

I sprinted down the hill, huffing and puffing. I heard the man's screech behind me. Then the man made a giant leap and tackled me to the ground. We both slammed into the ground, and started to roll down the hill. I punched my gun into the man's face, and saw a quick burst of red before the man let go. I slid down the hill, and quickly aimed to the man's head. The bullet connected with half of the man's head, which exploded. But the man screeched and got up, now a chunk of brain slowly slipping out of the damage.

"What the skup!" I yelled. The man screamed, showing the teeth, and then started to run toward me again. I popped another bullet into his chest and started running. The man sprinted behind me. The leaves flew back as I sprinted. The man took another jump as we ran. When I heard his feet leave the ground I took a leap too.

I jumped over a tombstone and landed on the other side. I turned and saw the demon hit the other side of the stone, dust exploding with a wet blob of blood fly above it. I got up and started to run again, knowing that this thing would not stop. I heard its screech and it crunching leaves to get up.

I weaved in and out of tombstones, trying to get away from this thing. Before long I heard its screech slowly become a fade in the distance. But I knew that it would continue to pursue me. I knew this cemetery well. I knew that in the very front there is a small cave made out of rock. And if I go far enough back, it won't be able to see me.

I ran to that position and right as I saw the cave, I ran harder than I ever had. I started walking when I got into the rough interior of the cave. I sat down, my back to the hard stone. I tried hard to steady my breath; I did not want that demon to be able to hear me. I could hear my heart pumping in my chest as I tried to figure out what the hell was going on.

What was this thing? It was like a demon. Is this what wanted me to become part of its "system"? What is going on! I missed my old life, and now this freak show has replaced it. What was going on!

Then I wondered if this was all a dream. Was it, how could I know? I usually know when I'm in a dream, and this did not seem like one. This was too realistic. Too long, too terrible. What would I do! The man said that this was his reality, so how can I get back to mine? And what the skup did he mean by reality? WHAT IS GOING ON!

Just then I heard the demon's screech. Oh crap where was he? It sounded as if he was close, but the cave did things to sound waves. I kept one hand on my gun, ears listening to every sound, eyes at the opening of the cave.

I saw the man before I heard him. Half of his head was gone; all that remained was one eye and half of his nose and mouth. Warm, sticky pieces of brain slowly flowed out of the wound. I kept the gun pointed at his head, waiting to pull the trigger. The man continued to walk.

As the man entered the cave, I waited for just the right moment. Then the man screeched, opening his mouth and sending blood out of it. Then I screamed and pulled the trigger. His head instantly burst into blood on the walls. His body stood there, like an active volcano, spitting blood out of the top. Then his lifeless body fell to the ground.

I covered my nose as the smell of death entered my mouth. I took a step back and put the gun into my pocket. Still covering my nose, I stepped over the body, allowing the blood to fill the cracks of the cave. As I stepped outside, I had a terrible thought. What if there was more of him out there? This was his reality, right? I don't want another demon man to come for me again. I already knew that my car was gone; I did not see it when I ran down the hill.

I slowly walked out of the cemetery. The sign that once bore "HAARP CEMETERY" was now half gone, and rusted. Leaves blew across the grass like they were being clashed by blood-spitting zombies. Which they might, I had no idea what was in this reality.

As I walked out of the cemetery, I spotted the first car. It was destroyed; all that was remained was scattered metal and a destroyed steering wheel. Outside of the cemetery was a straight street, usually full of houses on either side with playing children. Now all the houses were either caved in, or gone completely with only burnt wood remaining. The street sign that once said "MK AVE" was now destroyed, and was now just a metal pole sticking out of the ground.

As I came upon the first house, I noticed a tree growing through the middle; I kicked down the front door. It fell right off of its hinges. Once it hit the ground, it was like it fell into a body of water. Dust flowed out either side. The sound was loud and shattered silence. I looked around me to see if I attracted anyone. There was no sound except for my breathing.

I walked inside, struggling to see, the windows were covered by blankets that were nailed onto the windowpanes. I walked over to the first blanket. Since it was so old, I easily ripped it down.

The sun instantly revealed a dead body, long dead. Its chest was opened up, dried blood everywhere. Its face was gone, just dried blood and skin there for me to see. I slowly backed away. I expanded my vision, looking to the lighted room. Everything in the house was destroyed, broken lamps and tables scattered around. I left the house, knowing that I would not find anything there. I walked away from MK Ave, knowing that I did not want those images in my head.

I started walking down a road that ran alongside the right of HAARP Cemetery. Some trees were still standing, others fallen down to block the road. I saw a single raccoon run across the road, and then disappear into the cemetery. When I came to the end of the road I saw a corner store.

The door fell almost as easy as the last as I kicked it down.

"Hello?" I said quietly. The store was quiet. Dust flew around like fleas around trash. I panned my eyes around the empty building. All the shelves were broken, some gone with only spots on the floor to remember them by. I walked inside, looking for something, and found nothing. The glass cases built to hold frozen items on the left side of the store held a few metal bats, but nothing else. I opened the first case that I saw and grabbed a bat. It had the words MacGregor on the side in cursive. I closed the case and inspected it. Nice hard metal, dusty black paint job, the grey metal was starting to peek through on some spots.

I walked to the desk that was directly to the right of the store. I peeked over the side, and saw a blob of coats. I bend to pick one up, and when I touched it, the whole mass shuttered. I stepped back and watched in horror as the blob stood up. Then coat fell off, and I realized that it was a person.

The man yawned and stretched. He had a mustache and a bald head. When he was done he set down a big knife on the desk and another knife in his other pocket.

"What are you doing in these parts? You wanna get killed?" The man grunted.

"What do you mean?" I asked.

"You need to stay away from the bities." He responded.

"The what?" I said. The man laughed.

"The demons. I just call 'em bities cause when they get near you, they tend to get a bit bitey." The man said and laughed again. He had a hard British accent.

"Are you from Britain?" I asked.

"You know that there are no more countries. Just Land and Water." He said, inspecting his knife.

"What was done to the countries?" I said.

"What was done to the countries?" The man said.

"Ya." I responded. The man laughed. I just stood there, bat in hand.

"They were corrupted. By the bities," he said, laughing turned to frowning.

"Wait, what is the bities origin? How did they come to be?" I asked, now setting the bat on the desk.

"Well isn't that the million dollar question." He said, going back to cleaning his knife with a cloth taken out of his pocket.

"Why can't you tell me? I really want to know." I said.

"Ya, you and every other skupping survivor on this planet." The man said.

"What, so they just appeared out of thin air?" I said, using hyperbole.

"Pretty much. One second there weren't here, next second bam! The government is saying to stay inside. So I say 'the hell with them' and leave my apartment and run to the hills. I stay in a log cabin that I found. In a couple of months I return to find

everything as it was here. That was three years ago."
He said, the knife no longer his priority.

"Did you at least have a family to run with?" I
asked.

"I had a wife for around a year, and then we
broke up. No kids and I have no idea where she is."

"Melvin." I said, sticking out my hand.

"Chris." He stuck out his hand, and we shook.

"Now how do you kill these bities?" I asked.

"Take off the head, and their body will
completely disappear in a good day or two." Chris said.

"Like evaporate?" I said.

"Nope, their body will completely disappear.
Like, forever." Chris said.

"OK, so what have you been doing for the past
three years?" I asked.

"Walking, I usually find a place to stay like here.
I just walk. What else am I suppose to do? It's the

skupping post end of the world here." Chris said, smiling as he moved on the cleaning his second knife.

"How do you survive? Where do you get food?" I asked.

"I don't have to." He said.

"Why not? It's food and water." I said.

"I don't need any of it since I got this." Chris said and lifted up his sleeve. A bite was revealed, dried blood surrounding it.

"Did one of them bite you?" I asked.

"Yep. First time I saw one I thought it was a person. I asked it for help, and it bit me. So I got a brick and dropped it on its head. Got blood on my clothes." Chris said, scoffing.

"Are you sure that it isn't like a zombie bite, where you turn into one of them?" I asked.

"Don't you think that I would be one by now?" He said.

"Don't you think it would be healed by now?" I shot back.

"Smart boy. I have no idea. But either way, it makes me feel stronger and I don't have to eat or drink. I'm never hungry, never thirsty." Chris said.

"That's screwed up." Just then we heard a screech.

"Get the skup behind this desk!" Chris yelled. I dived behind the desk, and we both crouched down. Chris covered us with the blanket.

Then the thing burst into the store. I couldn't see it, but I heard it and smelled it. It smelled like a thing that comes in the night, like a burning pile of wood. I heard this crash and break. I heard the glass cases explode and the thing screech.

Then the blackness of the blanket was gone as the thing threw off the blanket.

"CCCCCCCCCCCCCCCRRRRRRRRRRIIIIIIIIIIIIIIIIIIIIIII IIIIIIIIISSSSSSSSSSSSSSSSSS!" it screeched.

"You skupper!" Chris yelled and took out a knife from his pocket and tried to stab it. But the thing quickly jumped back.

"Chris!" I screamed.

"Stay down!" he yelled as he dove over the desk, tackling the bitie. I stayed hidden with my back to the desk. With every crash or smash, I was tempted to look over to edge. But I stayed down like Chris commanded. Before long I felt both bodies of mass smash against the desk. Then I heard a squish and saw blood fly over the desk and land on the wall in front of me. Then it was followed by several of Chris' grunts and then there was silence.

"It's clear!" Chris yelled. I slowly looked over the edge. The demon was on the ground, stab marks all over its body. Blood was seeping onto the floor.

"Nice job." I said, not taking my eyes off of the dead thing.

"Oh, look. I have another one!" Chris said, pointing to his other arm. Now he had a bite on both arms.

"Oh, crap Chris. Are you sure that you won't turn now?" I asked, my eyes on the wound. But Chris did not answer. He just stared at the wound. Now the blood was flowing faster, and in chunks. It looked like a red slushie. That's not good.

"In the back of the store there are some paper towels. Get them and get this thing off a me." Chris said, not taking his eyes off of his arm. I sprinted to the back room. There were black shelves lining the walls. I spotted an unopened roll of paper towels and grabbed it. Then I quickly ripped open the plastic lining.

"Did this happen when you got your first bite?" I asked while ripping it open.

"I don't think so! Just get the towels!" Chris yelled from the other room. I finally got it open and sprinted back.

"Here," I said, handing the roll to Chris, flinging the plastic covering to the ground. Chris quickly wiped the slush-like red substance on his arm.

"Go outside and see if our little fight with the bitie attracted some more." Chris said.

"OK," I said and ran outside. I stuck my head out of the door. In front of me was a street, with random cars broken down in the middle of it. Then across the road I saw a demon sprinting toward us. It spat blood out its mouth and ran like a banshee.

I swore and reported to Chris.

"OK we need to get out of here, there's a back door in the closet that you were just in." he said, pointing.

"It seems that the slush stuff is gone." I pointed to Chris' arm, and then grabbed my metal bat.

"Ya must have been an automatic thing." He said, running with me to the back closet. We heard the demon bash through the door, wood splintering and glass breaking. We ran out a brown-painted door and into the back. A line of trees blocked our way to the back of a house.

"Keep going!" I yelled. We ran to the trees, but first closing the door. We ran over the broken branches on the ground and the random pinecones spread all around. I yet again heard the wood burst open as the demon ran through. We ran through the last of trees, and ran onto the porch of the house.

"I think I see a gun inside! Stay here and hold it back while I get it!" Chris yelled and jumped through the glass, landing on the carpet inside. He groaned from the damage and quickly got up. I looked at my surroundings. I was on a wooden porch, not very large. As I faced the woods to my right was a driveway with a parked blue Sedan. I pointed my bat over the wooden steps to the woods, where the demon was sprinting toward me.

The thing did not even use the stairs, he just jumped over them. I swung the bat, striking it in the face. The blood that was once in its mouth was now in the air. I swung once more, hitting it again.

"CHRIS!" I screamed. The thing kicked my stomach, making me fall to the ground. I slammed against the wooden porch and quickly made the bat parallel and pushed it against the demon's hands that were reaching for me.

Then the demon's head exploded, blood flying everywhere. I was given a quick shower of blood and warm sticky pieces of brain as the dead body fell on top of me. I pushed it off and looked behind me, spitting the foul-tasting blood out of my mouth.

"Look what I found!" Chris said, holding up a shotgun. I smiled.

"Maybe you could have shot him sooner?" I asked.

"Nah," Chris said jokingly. Just then a bitie burst out of the right glass door that Chris didn't break. It threw Chris to the side and ran toward me.

"MMMMMMMMEEEEELLLLLLVVVVVIIIIINNNNNN NNN!!!!!!" It yelled to me. I knew I should have recognized this house. It was Mark's, and the demon running toward me must be the now-bitie Mark.

"Skup!" I screamed, swinging the bat. I hit Mark in the chin, sending it flying to the right. I quickly ran to the left as Mark started to get up.

I jumped over the side of the porch and slammed into the top of the Sedan below. I rolled off, and continued to roll once I hit the pavement. While I was rolling I saw Mark land on his feet on the Sedan, jump off, and grabbed the front bumper. He then picked up the Sedan and whipped it at me. I rolled out of the way of the spark-throwing car swung past me.

"Did I forget to mention they're strong?" I saw Chris say, trying to aim the shotgun.

"Just focus on shooting it!" I yelled.

Mark then landed on top of me, and I went to bring up the bat parallel again, and then realized that I had dropped it when I ran off of the porch. I cursed and brought up my hand and grabbed Mark's throat. He made a quick gurgling sound then continued to attempt to grab me. His hands glazed my face, smearing it with blood as I pushed him away.

I looked past Mark to Chris. He was no longer trying to aim. The shotgun was in his hand, pointed to the ground. I could see him trying to do the math in his head. He had a gun now. He could either waste a bullet on saving me, or make a run for it and let me continue to distract the demon. So he ran, first off the porch and then to my right.

"CHRIS! NO! YOU BASTARD! NO!" I yelled at him.

"I'm sorry Melvin," he said but was interrupted by a bitie grabbing him from behind. The demon grabbed both sides of Chris' neck, and pulled. Chris' head came off easily and his decapitated body fell to the ground, spurting out blood. The bitie then took a chunk out of Chris' head with its mouth, brain matter on its lips.

"Serves...you...right!" I said, pushing Mark farther away. Then the demon that ate Chris dropped the eaten head and jumped over Chris' body to me. Crap.

I kicked Mark off of me and started to run out of the driveway. But I saw three more demons running my way, each coming from a different house. One looked like a forty-or so aged woman, one a teenage boy and the last a police officer. I turned around and saw the two other demons. I had to face five of them.

I turned around and faced the running Mark. When he came close enough I punched him in the face, and upon hearing the nose snap, turned around. The teen had arrived, and I brought up my foot to his face. He screeched and I turned and punched Mark again. Then the other four came around me, making a circle with me in the middle.

It's a good thing I took those karate classes when I was young. I gave the demons two roundhouses to the face and punched one more. As I fought, I was starting to get sweaty; I wouldn't be able to continue with this. I was going to die. I was going to die, and never know why the skup I'm here. Why was I taken out of my reality and put here?

Then I saw a bit of hope. When I kicked one of the demons (the police officer) I saw that the kick made his gun fall out of his holster. I pushed him back, and grabbed the gun. I didn't even check to see if it was loaded or not, I just pulled the trigger twice.

Two bullets slammed into the demon's head, blood exploding. I turned and sent two more bullets into the teen's head. It fell, revealing the other three.

I pulled the trigger again and nothing came out. I checked the ammo. I was all out, and behind me I could hear more screeches saying that there were more coming behind me. I turned and saw ten more running out of their houses.

"SKUP!" I screamed and threw the gun at Mark. It slammed into his head without a reaction. I looked past him and saw my metal bat lying on the ground. I ran through Mark and the woman and grabbed my bat. I swung around and smashed the woman's head.

I looked and saw more demons joining the ten. I looked to the road through the trees and past the country store, and saw around fifteen. This will bring the numbers up.

I swung the bat, smacking the woman. She fell to the ground. When her head smashed into the pavement, I brought down the bat repeatedly against her head. When Mark tried to grab me, I just pushed him away. The woman screeched and kept screeching, and I just continued to whack her. Eventually after a while of hitting her and adding to the blood on the driveway, she stopped moving. There was a giant gash deep into her head.

I pushed Mark aside and looked up. There were at least fifty of them surrounding the driveway, some on. Some were surrounding Chris' dead body, digging into the stomach, grabbing into everything that they can. That just wasn't right.

I ran and pushed away all of the demons that were blocking by way to Chris. All of them flashed their teeth and screeched. I screamed and started to back up. But I backed up directly into one of them, which threw me onto the ground. I got up and smacked it

110

with the bat. Then I ran to the flipped over car and climbed to the top of it.

The view was terrible. Now at least sixty of those things have gathered around the house. A whole group was surrounding Chris, like ants to a crumb. It was like a skupping town hall assembly here, I saw all types of faces.

Then one of them jumped up to me. I swung the bat and sent it back into the crowd. I turned and looked at the situation behind me. At least twenty. Three had started the climb up the car. I kicked one in the face, watched it fall, and then moved onto the others with the bat.

Once they fell, I turned to the other side. I was too late to bring up my bat before one jumped onto the car and tackled me to the other side. I collided with three other demons, sending them down with me.

I let out a silent scream and the bat slipped out of my sweaty hands. It rolled under the car as I slammed into the ground. The four demons quickly swarmed around me like a hive of angry bees. I tried to push them off, flinging them by the neck. I looked briefly past the car and saw the rest coming over to me. They jumped over the car and joined the group of hungry demons.

I continued to try to push them aside, but I had too little power. When I pushed aside a middle-aged man in front of me, one of them bit me in the head. My vision got blurred as blood poured down my face. It got into my eyes, and I automatically started to cry to clean them out. My vision was now gone, all but an extremely blurred image remaining.

As I blindly flung out my arm to hit any of them, one of them caught it and bit it. The once blurred image of my arm was replaced by red. I screamed as blood continued to fill my vision.

"Get the skup off of me!" I yelled to the crowd. But they continued to come. I randomly flung my arms and legs, trying to hit anything. But every time I tried, I got bit again. Blood was spurting everywhere, drowning me. I was choking on my own blood, dying by these beasts. But I was sick of it. Skup them. They think that they can just surround me and win? But how was I to win? How?

People say that before they die they think of loved ones and all that jazz. But I was thinking of how to get these sick punks off of me, to escape. I brought up my sleeve to my face as another one bit my foot. I wiped my eyes and screamed, my new view of everything showing me various bite marks all over me, blood flying everywhere, chucky pieces of meat in the demon's mouths.

It was then that I briefly thought of Gloria. I had always loved her...her short silky brown hair and her beautiful eyes. No, I wasn't going to die today.

I wiped my eyes once again and quickly sat up. I punched the one biting my leg and stood up, being surrounded by hungry hands. I punched two, sending the blood everywhere. Then I turned and kicked one with my good foot.

I grabbed one's head and sent it into another, kicked the one behind it. They started to close in, so I skupping closed out. I punched a skinny woman, and right after I grabbed her face, my fingers on her forehead. Then I threw her to the ground, and stomped on her head using my heel. My shoe immediately was covered in blood, as it hit the thing's eye.

The eye exploded into blood and the body stopped moving. I looked up and instantly got jumped by a demon. It tried to bring me to the ground but I threw it back. I was not getting on the ground again. I threw it to the ground and heeled its eye. More blood covered my shoe, but why do I care? I'm NOT dying.

I pushed one demon as it flashed its teeth at me. Then I brought up my foot and smashed its head. I saw three demons run to their dead kin on the ground and begin to flash their hands around, digging for flesh.

I looked up and was attacked by one of them that pushed me into the wall of the house. I smashed into the wall, and the thing started to try to bite my neck. I punched the side of its head, pointing its eyes to the ground. But it rebounded quickly and continued its quest for flesh.

Our hands were everywhere as I tried to get it away from me. But it continued to flash its hands all over me, trying to rip something open. I smashed its head again, its screech hurting my ears. Two other demons had gotten into either side of the one beating me, trying to get at me too. I smashed the first with my fist and felt a crack. I had broken its nose. Blood spurted out like a broken faucet.

I used this to my advantage. The two demons on either side were blocked by the first with the broken nose, so I had room. The broken nose was hurting the demon, and that's what I wanted.

I punched the nose again, sending blood to its new home on my fist. The thing screamed out in pain. My eyebrows narrowed, and I punched it again. My pinkie and index finger were smashing into the nose, the other finger used for leverage. The thing began to cry and continue to scream, tears mixing in with blood. I punched and punched again, adding my screams to it. Blood continued to spray out blocking my view. I screamed as I punched it. After its nose seem to have enough, I moved on to its head. I continued to smack it as hard as I could, use every bit of strength that I had. The thing cried out, but I gave it no mercy.

Then I stopped, and the thing did too. As it fell to the ground a terrible thought reached my head: did I just beat someone or something to death? As the demon-man fell to the ground, I realized that he had a life, a life that I had taken away as bloodily as I could.

As it fell I realized that I had fallen too. I had become an animal.

As the crowd of demons began to surround me yet again, my anger rose.

"WHAT THE SKUP IS WRONG WITH YOU!!! DO YOU WANT ME TO BEAT YOU TO DEATH TOO!!!!!!!" I screamed. I was responded by their screeches.

I kicked one weakly and it grabbed my leg. Without something to hold onto, I fell to the ground. As I fell, I saw that the demons had begun to eat their fallen comrades. Humanity really hasn't changed. Everything in life is basically eating one another. Putting each other down and lifting yourself up.

I don't know if I screamed when my head hit the ground. I don't know if I would have. I was too busy thinking about my life. My big screw-up life. About my poor mother, who I abandoned. She had raised me from the start, and now I've given up on her. It just wasn't right. I WILL survive. But not for me. For the people I've hurt, the people I've killed on the inside. The demon who I just killed was so easy to kill, so easy to do. This is how human nature was. I was so selfish, only thinking about me. Now I needed to think of my survival. My hopes and dreams were being destroyed by the fact that I was put into this reality, and I was never going to get out. What is wrong with me! There is hope! There is this life that I'm fighting for. But what is this life really? A chance for me to do whatever I want and not care about anyone else? What the skup is wrong with me! Life is a big race, and I wasn't running alone.

All this went through my head once I hit the ground. As the hungry hands started to close around me, I thought about what I could do. Nothing really. I was screwed big time. I could get up and fight them some more, but what was the point? What is the point of fighting anymore? I would never know. The hands were everywhere, and I could do nothing about it. Sometimes in life you just have to give up. But this is NOT my time.

I threw my foot up and barely glanced one of the demons and brought my second one up to kick another. I was not going to die. Not now, not now. But the demons did not agree with this. They constantly tried to eat at my soul, trying to bring me down. And my hands just flailing around would not stop them. Soon they would stop going for my head and realize that my legs were easy targets. But before then I kept punching them in the rough cheek as they tried to eat me alive.

But then one of them noticed my legs. And it went downhill from there. I had to choose to either protect my legs or my upper body, and I had to choose my upper body. The one demon sunk its teeth into my leg, pulling out a painful chunk of flesh and blood and sticky rope-looking things. I screamed, but I knew that I could never give up the fight with my upper body.

Then they started to get greedy and pull on my legs, then started to bite my thigh to try to disconnect my legs. This is NOT happening. I briefly thought about them taking away my legs, with my upper body all that remained. But I pushed the thought away, and thought about survival. I could not win. Everything was against me. Blood burst out of the wounds in my leg, and I yelled as I continually fought off the terrible things on top of me.

I started to cry. My life was leaving me. And there was nothing that I could do about it. My life was leaving me. I was about to die. And the worst part is that this was the seventh time I've thought this today.

That is way too many times today. This was not the way I wanted to live.

As the beasts bit and bit, tears streamed out of my eyes, mixing in with the blood. I screamed every time one of the demon's teeth sank into my legs, arms, or whatever. I tried to push them away, to get them away from me. But they did not want to be pushed away, they wanted blood.

Then I saw through my tears a demon jumping over its kin, a piece of intestine hanging off of its mouth. It jumped on top of me and I saw it reach out its teeth for my neck. Then everything went black.

Chapter 7

I blinked and everything was fine. I was at a circle table, a small one that was three feet wide. There was a red tablecloth with flowers stitched into it. A napkin was in front of me, and a wire chair across from me. I turned and saw that I was sitting in a metal wire chair as well. All around me were the same tables, most occupied by people in stylish t-shirts, and round hats.

I inspected my body. All the bites and scratches were gone, everything. What the skup? I felt my nose. It was back to normal, all normal-like. I looked at what I was wearing. My Muse logo t-shirt, the one that had a picture of the band with the logo in front. I looked around.

My table was exactly next to the street, when people walk by me they have to step aside my table. But the way that I was facing the café was to my left. It had a big sign that advertised it, and it was in a different language. Was this a different reality?

The café looked like it had no outside walls, it was completely open. The tables blended easily from outside to inside, looking like scattered polka dots. In front of the door was a stand with prices and food listed on them. I recognized the euro sign. So I must be in Europe.

I looked to my right. A busy street, full of cars speeding past, taxis honking at one another. Several restaurants were on the other side, also tons of office buildings. I heard voices, calm talking from the tables around me, and screaming on the street. I did not recognize the language, but the constant words that I heard were (I think) French.

A waitress walked over, dressed in white clothes. She started speaking in French, explaining specials or something like that, I had never taken French.

"Coffee?" I asked.

"*Oui, Oui.*" She said and walked away. Why the skup am I here?

Then I saw a man walk over, he was wearing a black shirt, with the Muse logo repeated multiple times, with various colors. He sat down in the chair across from me. He sat down with ease, as if he had been waiting for this and had arranged it from the start.

"Hello Melvin." He said, smiling.

"Robert Bellamy." I said with a cold stare.

"How are you on this wonderful France afternoon?" he asked.

"I'm in France?" I said.

"Yes, around three miles from the Eiffel Tower." He said back.

"Why and how am I here?" I asked right away. I wanted answers.

"I will get to that," Robert started.

"When?" I asked.

"Do you wish for me to start?" he asked.

"Very much so." I responded.

"What do you want to know?" he said.

"Everything there is to know. Everything." I said.

"I can tell you everything that pertains to the subject of you, but nothing else."

"So be it."

"Let's start with why everything has gone wrong for you before you went into reality check. Why was Jose shot and why did you lose your job just because you went to the police? Because what we were doing is not strictly legal in that sense. What we were doing in part was because of the government, yes, but a very small part. Our orders come directly from our leader, who gets them from the president. When I told you that one of the members on your ultimate frisbee team had a weapon of mass destruction, I was not lying. The thing is that it has something to do with the frisbee itself. We believe that the frisbee is some kind of device intended to do harm.

"When our team saw a poster for your first ultimate championship a while ago, we went to check it out, have a break from the entire ruckus of the government. While we watched, one of the guys from our team accidently brought his radio-wave detecting device. And it was going crazy inside his car. So we checked it out, and we were receiving high readings projecting from the area where the frisbee was.

"After that we followed your team around, hiding during your practices and games with our detector and other items. We quickly realized that the frisbee only released radio waves when it touched you, Melvin. So the person who brought the disc wanted to target you for some reason.

"We tried to get you in Exo-Politics, but you were nice enough to lock us in the bathroom. Then when we heard that you were brought into custody, we ran to the opportunity to communicate with you. We tried to talk to you privately about the subject, but we knew that you would not cooperate. So we used blackmail instead with your secret.

"Then you started to tell the police and we could not have our group be exposed. So we did everything in our power to stop you, including getting you fired. But you still would not talk to us. So we had to drastic measures.

"Time Warping was only used once or twice in our government, and it was relatively a new thing. And the government would do such a good job to cover it up, to hide it from the rest of the world. When one of us would go rogue and tell the world about our Time Warping, we would just say that they were crazy. So when we captured you to get information about the disc we used Time Warp to send us back a day or two, so if you were to escape, people would just think that you are crazy, you would see your other self, and believe it.

"Sadly you did escape though. It was then that we realized that you had a knack for escaping and surviving. Both emotionally with your mother or physically with robbers, you could get away, and you were fast. We realized that since you have played ultimate for so long you have not only gotten faster but stronger mentally. You could think about how to escape someone covering you, and think about how to get the disc no matter what.

"So we decided to use you on our latest assignment. We could not do it, because then our group will be exposed to the world. We could not let the CIA or FBI do anything about it, they're chumps. We had to take matters into our own hands." Robert finished.

"What the skup does that have to do with the demons?" I almost yelled.

"That's where we needed your help. You see, in the near future something bad will happen. And this happening will make humans become animals, demons as you called them. We saw that you were the perfect person to help us stop this from happening. So we got one of the demons from the future and brought it back with us, had you meet it, then sent you to the future with it. We needed to see if you could restrain these things, call it a test." He said.

"I don't get it at all. Why the skup do you need me to do it?" I asked.

"You'll find out soon enough Melvin. If I cannot explain it I guess that eventually you will see for yourself." He said.

"OK, well what is this 'terrible thing' that you say will happen?" I said.

"Someone will place a bomb on the base of the Eiffel Tower. Its explosion will have a strange effect on human nature. These new humans will not be the same that they once were. They will still have memories, yes, and know everyone that they did before. But all of their emotions will be gone. All of their emotions except one: anger. They will try, and try hard, to find and kill everyone that they know that is not one of them. Then once someone they know or one of them dies, they see it as a green light to dig in and have a feast." Robert explained.

"But how can this even be accomplished? How could a bomb do this? Your logic seems flawed." I said, trying to figure this out.

"Oh believe me, this is not something easy to understand. Not even we understand. Although we do know one thing: this is a very serious subject. And we need your help." He said, eyes locked on mine.

"So I guess that I will find out." I said.

"That's the spirit. Now before I go, do you have any more questions?" Robert asked.

"Yes, what's the date? Am I in the future?" I asked.

"Only two years passed since you got attacked in the tunnel, the exact month." Robert said and packed up his stuff. He then stood up, pushed in the chair, and walked away, disappearing into the crowd.

Then the waitress was back, and delivered my coffee. I heard that the service was slow in Paris. I looked around me. These people were not in a hurry. They did not have their ears clogged with cell phones or Bluetooths. As they walked, they seemed to enjoy life. Their eyes moving back and forth, realizing that every day is a gift. What the heck was wrong with us Americans? We spend every day like another day, not knowing that everything is different. If you ask a Parisian what they do, your answer won't be 'an accountant' or 'a secretary', but a painter or a singer. These people enjoyed life.

So why did it have to be Paris where the explosion would go off? I looked around and tried to picture all the faces around me being angry and twisted, blood dripping off of their teeth. It was hard, near impossible. But I knew that it would happen. Robert Bellamy sounded pretty serious.

But what if he was not right? What if this was all some kind of joke? But no, it cannot be, what could he have to gain? Making me run around screaming 'bomb' would only get me arrested and scare the skup out of everyone. Why did he want that? No, why *would* he want that? Since this did not make sense, he must be telling the truth.

As I sipped the coffee, I knew that he lied about one thing. He said that the demons were rid of all emotions except anger. That was not true. When I was viciously beating that one bitie, I saw the sadness in its eyes. It was seeing its life flash before its eyes, and realizing that its (more recent) events were all terrible. And it was so sad because of that fact.

But Robert did say that they did not get the chance to do extensive research on them. Did he say that, or was it just my mind imagining these things?

Just then my mind shifted back to my life before everything went skupped up. I wonder what everyone did while I was gone. Did The Musers still exist? If so, how were we doing? Did they replace me with someone else? Is he/she good?

I had left so much behind. What did Robert Bellamy's group of people tell everyone when I was 'Time Warped'? Did the government declare me dead? Kidnapped? What about my mother? Was she still alive, still leaving unanswered messages on my home phone?

During my entire life, I had given my mother nothing but grief. When my father died I guess I blamed her, and I do not know why. I guess when something goes wrong, humans must turn to someone to blame. If that is true, who was Robert blaming for this? Easy....the bomber. But who was that? A terrorist? Another branch of those that committed the 9/11 attack? Attack all sides of the Earth, start with America then move onto Europe? I had to stop these men. Or women, I did not really care, if these skuppers think that they can make a fool out of humanity, they must be thinking wrong.

But again my mind wandered back to the simple question: What did they have to gain? Turning complete humanity into flesh eating demons does not give you money or anything else. Well, it would be easier to rob banks and such, but why rob a bank when you can just as easily rob the store that you want to buy items from?

What if they did not know that this would happen? What if it is a new type of chemical bomb, a new type that they had no idea what it would do? Like when we bombed Japan, we had no idea what it would do, just that it would kill a lot of people, it would stop the war, and it would get the point across.

But what was that point? Just because we can kill and that we have big missiles means that we are better then everyone? That must have been what we were thinking. But was it the right thing to think? How could we ever know if it was?

I smiled, knowing that our species was certainly skupped up. And what could we do about it? Nothing. Except stop this bombing.

Another thing about the bombing: why couldn't they just do it? How hard would it be to just say 'STOP, BOMB!' Not very hard, I bet at least one of their men could do it. So why didn't they? Why was I needed to do this? Robert had some sort of secret agenda, and the only way to find out what it is, the only way, is to just hang with it. He wasn't going to tell me, so I was just going to have to find out by myself.

As I sipped the last of the coffee, the slurping sound that every five year old loves was emitted from the stiff plaster cup. Were there any kids in the post-apocalypse that I witnessed? None that I remember. Were they all eaten at the beginning? Killed by survivors, and then left to be scavenged by demons that were like vultures? It seemed that way. I could not let this happen.

"Check please?" I asked once I saw the waitress. She nodded and ran back inside. Once I saw that she was gone I sat up, pushed in the chair, and walked into the crowd, heading straight ahead. Hopefully the restaurant would not call the police for something as small as a $5 coffee.

As I walked down the street, passing shops and office buildings, my hypothesis was correct. These people just wanted to enjoy life. And who was I to stop them?

As I was walking I checked my pockets. Nothing in the left pocket, but in the right pocket of my jeans I found a Verizon cell phone and a wallet. I checked inside the wallet, and was greeted by dozens of Euros. Also inside was a crumpled-up note written on a lined yellow paper.

"Check into a nice hotel, get some clothes for yourself. We'll call with instructions. Don't get into trouble."

So it looks like I did have enough to pay the nice lady for the coffee. But I had already crossed multiple streets and walked by so many cafes, I don't think I would be able to find it again. And if I did, the service would be so slow I would probably still have time to sit back down before the waitress came with the bill.

I laughed to myself as I saw a familiar sign: A building with THE HYATT on the side. I crossed the street and walked through the revolving doors to the lobby. I was greeted with plotted plants and carpets engraved forever with revolving flowers. Gentle piano music played in the background over loudspeakers.

I walked over to the front desk, and was greeted by a man in a blue suit with a dark purple tie.

"A room for one please." I said.

"Yes sir." The man said, stroked his beard then typed into the computer. After a while he looked up.

"Oh, the name's Melvin. Melvin Pope."

"Well Mr. Pope, how many days do you wish to stay with us?" the man asked, looking at me with blue eyes. Forever, I wanted to say, but I had a job to do. How many days did Robert say until the bombing? Three days? I should do four just in case.

"Four days." I responded, taking out the wallet.

"Sir that will not be used. A man by the name of Mr. Bellamy has already informed me of a man with your name and description. Please, follow Michael to your room." The man said, smiling. Then the man gave Michael (who was sitting in a plush sofa on the other side of the lobby) a stern look, and Michael came running over.

"May I take your bags sir?" Michael asked.

"I would say yes, but I do not have any bags." I responded.

"OK then well sir just follow me." Michael said, and with that he turned around in his blue suit and purple tie and started walking toward the elevators.

"Please enjoy your stay!" The man at the front desk called out.

"Thank you," I responded back. Michael led me into the elevator and pressed the button on the side. The doors slowly closed.

"Your room is on the tenth floor." Michael said as the doors slid to a shut. Then as the elevator moved up, Michael kept his gaze on the metal doors, increasing the awkwardness.

As a familiar *ding* went off, the doors flew open, and I was greeted with a hallway with yellow walls (again with flowers) and a red carpet. Pictures of the Eiffel Tower lined the walls. Doors stuck out of the wall every ten feet, with a gold number above it, all in the hundreds.

"Right this way," Michael said, walking down the hall. I followed him, looking behind me to see if anyone was following me. I did not see anything except for the elevator doors slowly closing and moving back downstairs. I turned around and saw Michael standing next to a door on the left hand side. Number 114. Michael jabbed the room card into the slot and a green light went off and the door slowly opened.

"Wow," I said as the door opened. It looked plain at first. A dark room with black walls, a door ten feet across that opened up to a bathroom. On the left right next to that door was a closet. Michael continued walking, and I followed him. On the right was an opening in the wall that led to a large room with black walls, and a very big bed with red covers.

Then Michael walked over and opened the curtains. I was greeted by a fantastic view of the Eiffel Tower. It was almost glowing in the afternoon light. It was around a mile away, but the view was still grand. A little bedside table was on the right of the bed, with a lamp, a digital clock, and an *Entertainment Weekly* magazine, in English.

"There is a safe in the closet. Anything else I can do for you sir?" Michael asked.

"No thank you," I said, handing Michael five Euros.

"Here is your room key, thank you very much sir." He said, handed me the key and walked out the door, closing it softly. I looked at the key. It was decorated with pictures of flowers. Why the flowers?

I opened the curtains as far as they could go and lay down on the bed, staring at the white ceiling.

Then I remembered that I had something that I needed to do. I took the cell phone out of my pocket, dialed in a familiar number, and waited for the last ring. When the answering machine took over, I slowly spoke into the microphone.

"Mom, I am sorry for everything that I have done to you. I know that dad's death was not your fault, but I just needed someone to blame and I am sorry that it was you. Now mom, listen. I'm going to be away for a long time, and I may not come back. No matter what you do, do not call this number and do not call the police. And I love you, I love you very much and I'm sorry for everything that I did to you." Tears were in my eyes as I spoke. Then a click went off.

"Honey? Is that you?" An old voice on the other end said. I hung up, closing the phone. I stared to wail, tears running down my cheek. I could not do this. I threw the phone at the wall, and it hit it with a crack, and then fell on top of the TV against the wall, then to the ground.

I jumped off of the bed and ran to pick it up. As I was getting up I looked at myself in the mirror next to the TV. Tears were all over my face, and you could see the intensity in my eyes. This was crazy. I had to save the world. ME! Out of everyone in the world, he chose me.

But what did he say about the disc transmitting radio signals to me? What the skup was that all about? And why did he just move on from that to the world ending, like that was nothing. So I guess I just had to wait to get answers.

Then the phone rang. On the second ring, I flipped it open and pressed it to my ear.

"Hello?" I asked.

"How do you like your room?" A voice on the other end said, sounding like Robert Bellamy.

"I love the view." I said.

"You might want to put it on speaker; we have another briefing for you." Robert said. I pressed the button, put the phone on the bedside table, and sat down on the bed.

"OK," I responded.

"The bomb will be in a backpack. The backpack is orange with red stripes, do not mess this up. There will be thousands of backpacks there. The man who will drop off the backpack will not be Hispanic or Mexican, but looking like any other tourist. He will be a middle aged man, with a slowly balding head, skinny, a muscle-builder, around 5'2". He will be armed and dangerous. In the future with no one stopping him, he still took out a handgun, and has more guns in his backpack. He will have backup all around, armed and looking normal as well. You will never know who is a real tourist and who is terrorist." Robert said.

"When will this happen again?" I asked.

"Today is the seventeenth. It will happen on the twentieth." Robert responded.

"And how the skup am I suppose to stop him? Just yell bomb?" I said.

"Nope, that never works. A gun will be delivered to your room on the nineteenth." Robert responded.

"Why so late?" I asked.

"We want you to have some fun here in Paris."
Robert said. I could hear his smile on the other end.
There was something that he was not telling me. But I
would have to learn to just go along with it.

"Anything else?" I asked.

"Nope, just get yourself some clothes. I hear
that there is a store down the street that sells nice
Muse clothes. And have some fun; you are in Paris for
goodness sake." He said, and then hung up.

I closed the phone on the little table and picked
up the magazine. Some actor that I did not care for
was on the cover. I placed it back down and walked
over to the window. The streets were crowded and
people walked into random shops and other buildings.
This place would be in ruins if I did not do something
soon.

I walked back downstairs into the lobby then
outside to the warm Paris weather, my wallet and cell
phone in my pocket. I walked across the street to the
line of stores and walked into the first one that I saw. A
sunglasses store.

Then I saw the perfect pair of sunglasses. A cool wire frame, black with a holographic red stripe running through the middle. The frame itself was constantly changing colors, according to the light. I picked them up and looked at the price. A bit expensive, but skup it. If I was going to save the world, I would do it in style. I bought them, and with inspecting the rest of the store, walked outside, glasses on. The world seemed just a bit darker, not too much, which is what I liked. I walked to the other stores and got an assortment of clothes and one jacket for possible cold weather.

I walked back to the hotel and into my room. It took me a couple tries, but the door finally accepted my key. I walked in, put my bag of clothes on the ground, and lay down on the bed. Robert lied about the Muse store. That punk, I wonder what else he lied about. Someone on my team having a weapon? Ya right. Those were just normal guys, with normal lives. Or were they serial killers underneath?

I turned over and looked at the clock. It was getting late and all this shopping was making me tired. Then there was only one thing to do: party. See all the bars and clubs in Paris, go crazy.

I grabbed my jacket and my sunglasses, threw both on, and went back downstairs. The night was slowly growing dark. As I walked down the steps, then took a right into a small park, a small fair was inside the park, Ferris Wheel up and moving. There were little game tents everywhere, lights blooming. Kids ran around, going to each station, emptying their parent's wallets.

I walked quickly through, wanting to move from the children's play place to the adult's play place. As I walked through the park, past the fair, I saw a couple scary faces in the crowd, watching me. But I just kept walking, away from danger, for now.

As I came to the party district, lights flashed everywhere. Now this is where I wanted to be. Girls and guys lined the streets, wearing crazy outfits. Oh the French. I walked into the first bar that I saw, its name in French. I sat down at the bar, and asked the bartender for whatever was good here. He smiled and nodded, I think he understood what I said.

I turned around, observing the bar. Red and green lights flashed everywhere, under tables, on the walls, everywhere. It was like a Christmas party. The bartender came back and gave me a glass of brown liquid. I took a sip, it was sweet. I smiled.

A man walked over and sat on the stool next to me.

"How's it goin'?" the man said, and asked the bartender for a drink.

"Not bad. You?" I responded.

"Got kicked out of the house again." The man said. He obviously came here to blow his troubles away. I wish I could do that. He had short brown-blonde hair, and glasses with a short face. He was wearing a red jacket.

"Well then you are in the right place." I said, raising my glass for a toast. He raised the glass that was just given to him and we clanked glasses.

It went from there.

At around three A.M. I finally walked out of the bar. The man's name was Jack, and he sure could party. We drank, danced with some ladies, and other things. But as I walked back, I was a bit tipsy. As I stumbled into the hotel, then to my room, I had Jack's number in my pocket. We planned to meet in the same club then go exploring. I lay down on the bed; my last memory before drifting off was the clock saying four A.M.

I woke up and hit myself for falling asleep with no covers on top of me, and in my clothes. I looked at the clock, it was around 1 P.M. At least I got a good night's sleep. Just two more days until the bombing. I changed my clothes and ran downstairs. Then once I passed by a decorative mirror, I ran back upstairs. I looked terrible. I needed a shower.

After my shower I did not only look clean, but felt clean. I went back downstairs and went out to greet the day. But I needed breakfast. I looked at my watch, and then realized that I did not have a watch.

After I bought a watch I checked it. Time for lunch. As I was walking I saw the café where I had "appeared" in this time, where I had spoken with Robert Bellamy. I sat down and ordered lunch by pointing at the menu. I looked at the watch I just got. Nice metal, white all around. I looked through my sunglasses at the surrounding area, and saw a couple papers stapled to the café wall. I slowly walked over and read them.

"ULTIMATE FRISBEE CHAMPIONSHIP! AT JARDIN DES TUILERIES PARK BESIDES THE HYATT TODAY AT 5! TWO TEAMS, ONE VICTORY! COME WATCH THE TAKERS VERSE THE MUSERS!"

I knew someday we would make it to the championships. As I sat back down I looked at my watch. It was already 2:30. If I eat quickly I might be able to make it. But who was I kidding? The guys would attack me with questions about where the skup I have been and why have I shown up in Paris. This may not even be The Musers of America. It could be a French team for all I know. And I had a world to save.

My sandwich arrived and I dug in. As I did I thought that I was being extremely selfish. Just because I was chosen to save the world did not mean that I am better than everyone else. Or does it? Again I thought why I was chosen for this. What have I done to anyone?

I finished up and asked for this bill, this time planning on paying. When it came I left enough Euros for the tip as well. I opened up my wallet and looked inside. I had enough money to go on another shopping spree if I wanted to. Mr. Bellamy has taken very good care of me.

I walked back, planning on exploring the big city, or at least looking at the monuments. I walked down the street to my hotel, planning on walking through the park Jardin des Tuileries next to it. I know that a couple of monuments are just a step away from the park, like the *Arc De Triumph*.

When I finally got to the park, I realized that after looking at the monuments I could go to the Louve and check out the Mona Lisa and others. But first I wanted to see the Eiffel Tower.

Chapter 8

I could see it before anything else. It was looming over all of the trees, blocking out the sun. It looked like an array of twisted blocks of metal, but it was more than that. It was amazing, so tall. When I finally walked over to it, I realized how big it actually was.

The Eiffel Tower was so big; it was claiming its glory over me. Tourists ran all around the pavement under it, struggling to get a picture. But I did not notice them. I was too busy noticing the pure glory of the Eiffel Tower. I could not grasp how big it was. Then my eyes slowly moved down as I walked under it.

People were all around me, some people laying out mats trying to sell mini plastic Eiffel Towers. I walked past them, staring above me, mouth open. It was just so vast, so amazing. I ran to the nearest leg of the Tower to buy tickets to go up.

I bought them, went through the line and into the elevator. Twenty more people joined me, and we rolled up. When it stopped I was the first one out. We were on the first observation deck.

As I walked out the first thing that I saw was the restaurant. Then I saw the fountains spitting out water. Then I saw the chairs and tables. I ran over to the railing and looked at the view. Oh, Paris. The view was spectacular, I could see everything. France was everywhere, surrounding me. I felt so tall, so awesome that nothing could hold me back. I could not let this place be bombed, because then how could everyone get the same awesome experience as me? This was not going to be bombed. No skupping way.

But then as I looked over fabulous Paris, the skis began to darken and rain began to fall. Even though the big mass of metal above me was huge, it did not block some of the water that dropped from the sky. I took off my glasses and looked up as a raindrop flew into my eye. I quickly brought up my sleeve and wiped it off.

After that I turned around to see how everyone else was reacting. It was as if they did not care at all. They continued to eat their food, and talk around. But as I was looking into the crowd I saw something of interest.

A backpack. Not just any backpack, but the backpack that Robert told me to look out for. And the person carrying it was the same man Robert had said, with balding hair, middle aged. He was looking around, most likely observing. Was he going to do the bombing early? No, because Robert had gone into the future and knew when it took place. But then there was the possibility that he lied. He did lie about the emotions of the demons, so did he lie about everything else?

I must have been staring at the man for too long because he noticed me. Then he started to run. Standing still he was around twenty feet away from me, and his running was making this distance longer.

On the side that I was on, there were little stands with food and tables, with a couple fountains. Then in the middle of it all was a giant hole, leading down to the pavements of people swarming like bees below. Then on the other side of the hole, connected by two walkways of either side of the hole, was the big restaurant. On each leg of the Tower there were stairs leading down, and a ton of stairs at that.

Now the man was running to the left walkway, to the restaurant. I quickly started to follow him. I pushed people out of the way, and I got yelled at but I did not care. I needed to stop this man.

"HEY! STOP!" I yelled. I knew that he would not stop; I said it mostly to get people's attention and to encourage stopping him.

The man sprinted over the fake grass, me behind him. Since he was middle aged and I was an athlete, I was slowly catching up to him. But the man was obviously a runner, his form showed it. The backpack was slowing him down, but he would not give up.

As we ran past the informational signs bolted to the railing protecting the hole, I realized that the man was going for the staircase on the east hand side leg. If he goes inside an elevator when its doors are closing I will not be able to stop him. Fortunately there is a small chance of that happening. He will most likely head to the stairs, and in that case I will be able to stop him. I could just jump down and tackle him.

As he ran to the doors that opened to the stairs, I used a quick burst of energy to catch up to him.

He tried to shut the door on me, but I was there and caught it then jumped down the small flight of around ten stairs and tackled the man to the ground.

The stairs on down the Eiffel Tower legs were simple: ten steps down, little platform then a complete one hundred and eighty degree turn, then down ten more steps one hundred and eighty degree turn, and repeat.

As the man and I fought on the platform, he shook the backpack off of him, knowing that it would only slow him down. He then punched me in the face; my nose exploding in a burst of blood, then threw the backpack off of the side, sending it crashing to the ground. I got up and ran to the railing, looking over while covering my blood-caked nose. The backpack fell to the ground, then hit someone below on the head. The head was quickly blocked by a burst of blood, and then my vision showed me a woman lying on the ground, blood not only spraying, but sulking away like a snake in the grass.

The man used this as a distraction and started to run down the next length of stairs. I turned and ran down after him. He got down to the next platform and moved onto the next set of stairs as I finally reached the second platform. I looked around the platform and saw a rock as the rain continued to fall. I picked it up and turned to the man, who was on the third platform. I whipped it at the man; striking him in the head, a gash made causing blood to spew. He fell and I quickly ran down the stairs to catch up to his crawling body. I jumped on top of him, turning over his body.

I punched him once in the face, breaking his nose, sending blood into the air, the rain slowing wiping it off my fists for me. I tried to punch him again but he grabbed my fist and bent it back. I screamed as he pushed it past my pain limits.

"YOU CAN'T SKUPPING PREVENT WHAT IS GOING TO HAPPEN! YOU JUST CAN'T!" the man screamed. I screamed as he pushed really far back. He slowly stood up, knowing that he had the upper hand. As he slowly stood up, I pushed myself to stand up with him.

"Let...me...skupping...go!" I said to him, pausing to take breaths. We continued to rise as the rain poured down, adding to the intensity.

"No way. I'm gonna need to dispose of snitches like you!" he said and pushed me back against the five-foot tall railing to prevent people from falling. But it was not going to save me.

"Oh, skup no. Oh, you sick skup!" I yelled at the man.

"I told you to get the hell out of my business but you didn't listen!" he yelled, grabbing my feet and starting to lift me over the edge.

"You never told me that! Never once in my life!" I yelled back, greatly fearing my life was ending as he lifted my feet higher and higher.

"Well now I just did!" he said back. I looked over his head, trying to see if any tourists had heard my cry for help. The stairs were empty. I was so screwed.

When my body was level, I really started to freak out. I was screaming for help, but no one would answer my cries. It seemed that the whole Eiffel Tower was empty. As the raindrops poured down, I feared that I may be going down with them. My head would hit the pavement below first; causing an explosion of blood and warm pieces of brain, followed by screams, and the man would most likely go back up the stairs and leave the Eiffel Tower down another way. And then I would be dead, and the bombing would go on.

Then I saw my opportunity. The man briefly let go of my right leg, so I thrust it upwards into the man's face. He screamed and let go of my entire body. I slowly tilted back as the breath escaped my lungs, and my heart skipped a beat. I fell backwards, and time seemed to slow down.

"Oops," I heard the man say, but it sounded like it came from a distance. I fell back and back and it never seemed to end. I opened my mouth to scream, but nothing went in or out except for the falling rain, which now I joined as I fell to my death. I did not feel the man's hands try to save me; I think that he was as shocked as I was.

I quickly fell past the platform that I was once on, headfirst. The air breezed by me like a tidal wave, there but gone. It seemed like I was gaining speed as I went by, going faster and faster. I was going down with my head pointed to the ground, so there was no way that I could put out my hands to stop myself. The falling was pushing the air into my face, then all around.

I thought about how I could stop this. The platforms blew by, and I was getting closer and closer to the ground. Then I came up with an idea. I saw an elevator slowly moving up, and I was going toward it at very high speeds. I tucked my head into my legs the best that I could, considering the fact that I was falling, and braced myself for the collision. I closed my eyes.

My back slammed into the hard metal, and my breath escaped me. A sharp pain electrified through my body, causing me to try to scream out. My lack of breath prevented this, and I felt something snap. My body rolled forward, I was sliding off from the impact that I had made with the elevator. I quickly flung out my hand and caught onto one of the antennas that jetted out from the top. It bent a little, but it held.

My body screamed out for help as my legs just barely hung over the edge. But the antenna would hold for now. Once I got my breath back, I tried to pull myself slowly, holding onto the bottom of the antenna so it would not break. I slowly pulled myself up as the elevator went up at high speeds. When I was lying on top of the elevator catching my breath, I inspected for damage. From the obvious signs (my leg being straight and no bones visible) I could tell that I had no major damage. But no one could endure that maybe twenty foot fall and not at least hurt something. And there was that crack that I heard.

I opened my eyes wide and looked above me. The elevator was reaching its stop, and there was a slight roof over the doorway. That could be a problem if the elevator does not stop in time. Although I did have faith that it would. As we neared the small roof, I thought I might have to move. I moved an inch and realized that it would be harder than I thought. If I wince when I just move an inch, what will happen when I move a bigger distance? Nothing good, I'll tell you that much.

The top of the elevator passed by the clear doors that new passengers would soon go through, but as I looked through I saw that the tourists were too busy texting inside their rain jackets to notice me. The elevator slowly continued to inch toward the roof, slowing down. I knew that at this speed I would not be crushed, I would not have my blood mark the roof forever. I would most likely just be in a very uncomfortable position until the elevator goes down again. When my nose started getting pushed to my face, I realized that I was right. But the elevator kept pushing. My nose continued to push it, until I heard it snap and blood started to stream down my nose.

Of course a couple of seconds after that the elevator finally stopped. It couldn't have stopped a couple of seconds earlier for me to maybe, I don't know, not break my nose for a third time in a month? I was kept in an uncomfortable spot for at least ten seconds, and then the elevator started to move down again. As the elevator passed the stairs, I looked for the man. He was nowhere in sight. I lifted my arm up to message my broken nose, but every move strained my arm.

Then I realized that I would be stuck on this elevator. I could not move myself enough to get myself off of it, at least not for a little bit. I was stuck on this elevator. As it moved slowly down, I stared at the Eiffel Tower from below. I felt like I was one of the many people below, wishing that they could have enough money to go up. Every once in a while a rain drop would find its way past the barricades of brown metal, and find its way to slowly begin to wipe the blood from under my nose.

I do not know how long I lay on the roof of the elevator. All that I know is that I finally realized how far-fetched this whole thing was. I am not a CIA or FBI agent! I'm just a normal person! If I could not recover from a quick drop onto an elevator, how could I stop a skupping bombing! I couldn't, and I could never be fit to. This is someone else's job, not mine. Robert's people should be doing this, not me! Why just pick me off the street and fly me to Paris to stop this bombing, and expect me to believe all he says? He could be the skupping terrorist for all I know! Which I will never know! What the skup am I going to do!

I will call this whole thing off, that's what. I'll just press the call back button on the cell phone Robert gave me and call him back. Calling him back, I'll just say that I am done with all this crap and for him to book me the first flight back to America, home of the free. No, I don't need him. I still have tons of money inside the wallet he gave me, and I even heard someone come into my hotel room late at night to refill it. I had enough to buy the skupping Eiffel Tower that I was imprisoned in! OK, maybe not.

Either way, I was going to end this. He said himself (or at least implied it) that this would be easy. Just yell bomb and the authorities will do the rest. So why can't he do it! It does not make any sense! Why can't he just scream one little word and point one little finger at the man, then just run away. How skupping hard was it!

He just needed to man the hell up and do it himself! But then a little voice inside my head told me that's what I need to do. Just man the skup up and do it myself. This may not be my war, but if this threatened all these people, it was. But I knew that it was crazy. So, so crazy. But isn't this the one time in everyone's life that they have been waiting for? Everyone wants to be a hero. Now here was my chance, and it was slipping away. This was my chance, my chance at everything. Fame, fortune, all that jazz. But was it really true? Or just an illusion? Was Robert really expecting me to believe that someone on my team was doing experiments with me through the disc? That did not make any sense, therefore I dismissed it as nothing more than a myth. But maybe he was just saying that to make me trust him, that would make sense right? But what really made sense anymore?

A rain drop smashed into my eye, bringing me back to reality. I don't know how long I was on the top of the elevator, just that it could have been as short as five minutes and as long as an hour. I cannot believe that no one has noticed me yet. But if someone did, would they really do anything about it?

I slowly sat up, a pain jabbing my back. I winced, as the pain slowly subsided. I then looked around me. The elevator was slowly going up as I passed by various metal platforms. Could I jump to one of them? No, jumping would be too risky. But I could roll off. I may not be able to see where I was going, but I could just wing it. If I roll fast enough, I would most likely cover the five or so feet that I had to cover before landing on my back on a metal platform. And if I missed the platform I was aiming for and hit the fence, my body would just automatically land on the next platform below it.

I looked over one last time. I set my aim for the metal platform that we would pass in a couple of seconds, laid down, and rolled. I closed my eyes, and right after my body left the elevator my heart skipped a beat. My breath was lost, and I flew through the air. Then my back smashed into something metal and my eyes flew open. I was on the metal platform, and I watched as the elevator went up beside me. I had made it.

I tried to get up, and winced as my back groaned. This was going to take some work. I took in a big breath and sat up. Then I braced myself and stood up. My legs felt a little stiff, but nothing that I could not handle. But then what was that cracking I heard? I did not feel any broken bones. As I stood up, I did not feel anything out of the ordinary. So it must have been my knuckles cracking or something. That was OK, as long as I did not do any damage to my fingers.

I felt my nose. The blood had stopped running, and the blood on my face was now dried. I must look like a crazy person, dried blood all over my face and dirt all over, cuts all over my body.

I slowly continued going down the stairs, hand on my waist, limp in my left leg. I slowly moved down the stairs, making my way down. How many stairs were there? I know that I had learned it sometime in school. It seemed to have left me now. Not that it mattered. All that I knew is that it was a long way down, and I had a limp to deal with.

As I limped down, various people ran past me, energetic, almost sprinting up. A group of kids ran by me, speaking in French. Why hadn't these people gone up when I was on the elevator? Or fighting the man? Sometimes I just hate irony. If they had climbed up the stairs just a bit earlier, then maybe they could have called the authorities to save me. Just maybe.

When I finally got to the bottom, I feared the swarming crowds. I feared that some stupid French kid would kick my foot, or because I am not moving fast enough I would get pushed down. As I reached the last step, I observed the crowd and stopped. It looked like the ocean, with bobbing heads like waves all around. I peered over everyone and saw that the only way in or out was pushing others out of the way. I could not do that with my leg, no skupping way.

I looked behind me, behind the leg of the Tower. There were a couple of bushes, and when I looked closer, a walkway. Perfect for me. I limped down into the crowd and took a hard right to the walkway. I pushed aside multiple people, but they were walking so fast I bet that they did not even notice me. I limped over to the walkway, full of rocks and random ditches that were slowly filling up with water as the rain poured down.

The puddles exploded as I hurried through. I limped as quickly as I could to the next street and waved my hand for a taxi. One stopped and the door flew open. I told the man the name of my hotel and we drove off. As we drove through Paris, rain drops smashed against the window. People's faces completely disappeared as a rain drop smashed onto their faces, or so it seemed through the window.

I watched as our taxi slowed down in front of the hotel, and a man all dressed up in a suit and tie opened the door with one hand, the other holding an umbrella.

"Thank you," I said, getting out and handing the driver money and said the same to the man dressed up for the hotel. I shut the door behind me.

"*Bon* Jour. Do you have any luggage?" The employee from the hotel asked.

"No I am good thanks." I responded, and passed the man into the hotel. But he stopped me before I could reach the door, as the taxi drove away.

"Sir, I see that you have a limp. Should I send up medical personnel to your room?" he asked, concern in his eyes. I thought about this. Medical personnel would be able to help, and hopefully get me ready for saving the world in two days.

"Sure, thank you." I said. I told him my room number and went inside. The windows on the side of the lobby were no longer letting in perfect sunlight, but darkness, and raindrops on the glass. I walked over to the elevator and summoned it. The light blinked and I realized how easy it was to get accustomed to living the high life at a hotel. I don't have to use the skupping stairs, because I'm that important. Life is funny how it changes.

The doors opened and I walked inside, there was no one there. I pressed the button to close the doors, then my floor number. There was no elevator music, just the sound of rubber breezing against metal. Then the doors slid open on my floor. I stepped out, and walked to my room. I opened my wallet to get my room key, but the door was already open. I looked around the hallway. There was no cart with cleaning supplies, so it was not housekeeping.

I slowly walked inside, keeping my step noise to a minimal. Since the floor was a carpet, this was easy. The bathroom door directly in front of me was empty, so no one was in there. I slowly turned the corner to the bedroom. No one was there.

Then someone jumped out from behind the corner. Someone I would have never expected to jump out, not in a million years. She screamed, and then I screamed.

"Gloria, what are you doing here?" I asked. She stared at me.

"I don't know. I just got a plane ticket in the mail to come here. So I thought, Paris! So then I came." She said, smiling.

"Well it's good to see you." I said, and we hugged just about the most awkward hug I have ever had in my entire life.

"I like this hotel and the view." She said, looking around the room.

"How did you know what hotel and room that I am in?" I asked.

"I didn't. Some guy at the front desk told me that you were staying here, and if I knew you, so I said yes." She said, brushing aside her beautiful hair. I tried not to stare.

"Wanna go for a walk?" She asked.

"Sure," I said, blushing.

"I just have to call the front desk and clean up a little." I said, and ran over to the phone.

I told the front desk to delay the medical personnel until later tonight. They agreed and I set down the phone. Gloria was standing by the door. I walked around the corner, ready to tell her about the sights of Paris and how much fun we would have. But when I turned the corner, there was a Hispanic man with his one hand around her mouth and another one around her neck. I gasped.

"Let her go." I said quickly.

The man slowly shook his head and took off down the hallway, closing the door behind him. I quickly limped over to the door to try to catch it before it shut, but I was too late. The door shut and automatically locked. I swore and fiddled with the locks to open it. Once it was open, I ran through, and looked for the man and Gloria. I saw the doors to the stairs slowly close. They went down that way. Seriously, more stairs today?

I pushed open the door to the stairs and looked down. There were tons of metal stairs going in circles all the way down the ten floors. I looked down, and saw the man and Gloria halfway down. The man was fast for holding and dragging a hostage. He had obviously done this before. So was this all a plan, bring Gloria down here and threaten me?

I ran down the stairs, even though he was fast I knew that I was faster. Around and around I went, down the stairs. I saw the man go through a door at the bottom, a door labeled "STAFF ONLY". I caught up and tried to open the door. It was locked.

I tried to push it open as hard as I could, but there was only so much I could do considering the fact that my whole body was sore from the fall today.

Then I heard the door click a couple of minutes later and I burst through. As the door closed behind me I did not see a pretty sight. I was in a loading dock, and Gloria was tied up in a chair and three men were standing around her, including the man that took her. They were all wearing typical Parisian clothes, t-shirts and jeans. Gloria had on a mask over her face, so she could not see anything.

"What do you want?" I asked.

"We'll be the ones asking the questions. Just know that if you move, she dies." One of the men said, the one farthest to the left.

"Then ask away!" I said, angry.

"How did you get to Paris?" he asked.

"I honestly don't know." I said. The man smiled and took something out of his back pocket. It was a crowbar.

"We don't have to do this," I started, but I was too late. The man flung down the crowbar, striking Gloria in the arm. Blood splattered. She screamed and I did too. Her white dress was instantly drowned in blood around the arm, and it was slowly moving down her arm. She screamed again.

"I will ask you again." The man said.

"I told you," I said, tears streaming down my cheeks, "I don't skupping know."

"So be it." The man said, and struck down the crowbar again. The other two faces remained silent and still. This time he hit her other arm. Blood burst out. She screamed again. This was just too much. I started to run toward her.

"George?" the man said. The man who captured Gloria ran up and grabbed my arms, sending pain through my body. He put them behind me and did not let go. I screamed out for help but no one heard. I watched as the man repeatedly used the crowbar, striking Gloria in the arms, and then moving down the legs. Her once white dress was now soaked with blood.

The man asked me one more time if I knew how I'd got here. I answered the same: I did not know. The man smiled. I asked him to please stop, to please find it in his heart to stop skupping hurting people. The man found this amusing. He mentioned to the man standing next to him how much he hated Gloria's screams. I greatly feared where this was going.

"I swear if you skupping touch her!" I yelled.

"Then I guess we're going to hear some dirty words." The man said as Gloria screamed through the mask. He then struck down with the crowbar, and everything seemed to go in slow motion. The crowbar hit the top of Gloria's head, and she screamed once more. But as the crowbar went farther and farther down, as the blood continued to flow out like a water fountain, her screaming stopped. I yelled out her name, George held me back from attacking his friends.

The crowbar continued to go down, even though I thought that it could go down no more. Blood exploded out, included with chucks of whatever no one should ever see. The man's clothes were now nearly soaked in blood. I tried to close my eyes, but George's hands reached down and forced my eyes

170

open. Through barely opened eyes, I saw the man continue to attack Gloria's limped head, part of the skin including her hair starting to fall off, landing on her lap.

I yelled out her name again and again, but it was clear she wasn't going to be answering me. The man struck the crowbar again and again, and eventually it seemed that her corpse had run out of blood. The man stopped, catching his breath.

"Well that was fun wasn't it?" he said, a huge smile on his face and pieces of brain on his shirt.

"You sick piece of skup! SKUP YOU!" I yelled out, staring at the body. Her mask was now off and her eyes were open, as if she was in shock.

"We brought her here for one reason. To show you that we don't want any bullcrap." He said, staring at me.

"What the skup do you want?" I screamed.

"We want you to just go home, and forget about all this. You never met Robert Bellamy; you never met anyone who gave a crap about the Eiffel

Tower bombing. And if you don't, it'll be your mother in the chair next time."

"You wouldn't," I said, glaring.

"Oh, I would. Tickets to Paris to reunite with her son? Who wouldn't jump to that opportunity? I think that it would be a fun time." He said.

"You stay the hell out of my personal life. SKUP YOU!" I yelled.

"Then why don't you get the hell out of international affairs? You are not a superman! You worked at a Best Buy for skup's sake! You have no life. Don't start one now." He said, now raising his voice.

"THE HELL WITH YOU! IF THIS IS SOMETHING THAT THREATENS HUMANITY, IT IS MY PROBLEM!" I yelled back.

"Nice nose buddy. Want me to add to it? I wonder if we'll be able to see the difference between Gloria's blood and yours!" he yelled, waving the crowbar.

"You think that you can set off a bomb and everything will be OK? Well I got some news for ya. It won't! You will turn humanity upside down! Humans will become mindless demons looking for flesh!" I screamed, trying to make my eyes avoid the corpse.

"And how the hell do you know that!" he asked.

"I overlooked the bomb, and that's what my reading said." I lied.

"Well, you don't think that we thought of that! You think we're stupid!" he screamed.

"You must be considering the circumstances." I replied. The man stared at me.

"You may think that the world will never recover from this. Stuck up on zombie movies aren't ya? You think that the government will just fall don't ya? Well you're wrong. The only thing that will happen is that everyone will be freaked out for a couple of months, and then everything will be put under control." He said.

"No, you don't understand! It'll go on for years!" I said back, revealing my knowledge.

"And how do you know that?" he asked.

"I...have a hunch." I lied. I could not tell him how I really did know.

"Exactly. Everyone will be freaked out for just a little bit, and then the army will take care of everything. People only having anger as an emotion will not be that hard to kill, believe me." He said, smiling. He made the same mistake that Robert did, saying that they only had one emotion: anger. But that was a lie, a lie that they shared. Was it a coincidence? This was getting way deeper then I feared.

"Whatever you say." I said.

"Ya know what? Skup you. I'll let you go, and you can carry on with your life. But after the bomb goes off, and you die with it, we'll send someone to take care of your mother once and for all." He said, and George let me go. I brushed off my arms. George walked over and met the other two men, and they walked out of the door in the back on the concrete-walled loading dock.

"I'll see you in two days." He said, and then walked outside.

I stared at the body. Skup them, I was going to prevent this bombing. One way or another, their plan would not go on. I will stop them. I don't care if they kill anyone else, this was my war. And if they wanted to hurt me, they could hurt me. But not my friends, not my crush, and not my mother. This was about to go down, and go down hard. I was angry. Skup them.

I turned around and walked out of the loading dock, up the stairs. This was getting intense. Maybe too intense for me. But what was too intense? It did not seem that getting jumped in the tunnel was too much. Or what about Jose getting sniped and getting tortured? What about the minutes I spent fighting the mass of flesh eating demons, or even getting dropped from the Eiffel Tower? What was too much for me? Was there even such thing?

I am just a normal man, but I guess no one is normal. What is going on with my life? Every single person that I met in this life was getting closer and closer to my secret. It is not long before someone exposes it, and then the entire universe would be in danger. It is a secret for a reason, and I trust that the people who already know it will keep it secret.

I finally got to my room. I had left the door swung open, and as I stepped in, memories of Gloria passed through my head. Her silky black hair, moving from side to side-what the hell was wrong with me! This is just as physical as it was mental. I needed to keep a level head. And if that meant not mourning over the loss of my crush then so be it.

I closed the door behind me and opened up the blinds, sat down on the bed. The Eiffel Tower was all lit up, the sun gone and the sky turned to night. The cars ran around in the streets below, lighting up like bulbs on a Christmas tree.

I grabbed my cell phone, got Jack's number from the drawer, and called. I left a message saying that I got injured and could not complete our plans and to just go and have a good time without me.

Then I put the phone down and picked up the hotel phone to call for the medical personnel, but then stopped. I did not need their help, and all this running today had pretty much put everything back into its place. I was better than I would ever be. Although I had tomorrow off, then the day after I had to save the world. What would I do tomorrow? Most likely rest, get ready.

I changed into some pajamas that I bought earlier, and dropped my clothes in the trash. They were ruined due to the day's activities. Then I put all of my bags with the new clothes in the closet, including the stuff that I got from the electronics store. I hope that I would never use them, as it would expose my secret. And I promised myself to use it only when necessary. I then turned on the TV to some English news station and rolled into bed. With the big covers over me, I was thankful that I already turned off all of the lights. I lowered the volume slightly on the TV and drifted off to sleep, preparing myself for the intensity ahead.

When I awoke, I turned over to look at the clock. It was around eleven in the morning, and I was still groggy. So I closed my eyes again.

When I awoke again, I knew that I was really awake. Something about me did not want to go back to sleep. I sat up, and looked at the TV. Some soap opera was on, and it was quite comical with the English accents. I chuckled a little and looked over to the clock.

It was already mid-afternoon. Wow I slept late. I slumped out of the heavy covers and walked over to the window, and flew open the blinds, exposing the busy Paris streets and the beautiful Eiffel Tower.

Chapter 9

These streets were busy with life. Busy enjoying their life that, if I don't do anything, will be thrown into chaos. This is going to be good, and I had no idea how it will turn out. Tomorrow will decide how everything turns out. Tomorrow either I will save the world or everything will go as normal, or the first demon would be created and the world will crumble and die.

For that entire day all that I did was order room service, and watch TV. It actually was not that hard. I left my room once to eat dinner in the fancy dining room downstairs. Then the next day when I woke up, I was ready. Today was the day, the day that I would either save the world, or completely destroy it.

They say that life is precious. "They" are right. But it is not only your life that is precious; everyone else's is just as precious. They have sons, daughters, parents, everything. You are not the only important one here. And now that must be decided by me. This could come down to me sacrificing my life for the world. Would I really want to give it all up? What was I giving up anyway? Ultimate Frisbee games and bar visits afterwards? Was that really what my life was all about? I did not have any next of kin, any brothers or sisters. All that I had was my mother, and I had made my peace with her.

Then the cell phone rang behind me on the bedside table on the right side of the bed. I leaned back and grabbed the phone.

"Hello?" I asked.

"This is Robert Bellamy." A voice said on the other end.

"Let's get this going", I said.

"You know the gun that we promised you?" he said.

"Yep." I said back.

"We have it for you. Go outside of your room to the left of the elevators is a door to some stairs. Go all the way down, and there will be a door at the bottom that leads into the loading dock. There one of my men will have the gun for you." Robert said.

"It's that easy?" I asked.

"It never is. We have word that someone might try to disable you." I gasped. "But don't worry. We will have men down there to protect you. Do you have a flashlight in your room?" he said.

"A flashlight?" I said, confused.

"To further disable the enemy, we will try to confuse them by turning off the lights."

"So we'll be in complete darkness?" I said, astonished.

"Yes."

"But if I'm waving a flashlight around, wouldn't the enemy know where I am?"

"That's why my men will also have flashlights."

"Dude, this is intense."

"My men will see you down there in one hour. Then, after that, you need to go straight to the Eiffel Tower. I will hope to have figured out the time of the bombing attempt by then, and I will call you when you get your gun and come back to the room."

"OK, see you then." After that I hung up, and placed the phone on the bedside table.

I needed to change out of these pajamas, into something else that I hadn't worn for an entire day. I threw the pajamas into a plastic bag that I found in the closet. Then I put on the clothes that I found when I was eating in the café, the clothes that I wore when I first came to Paris. Muse t-shirt, blue jeans. It was only right that what I wear into Paris, I wear out of Paris.

An hour later I was ready to go. I ran out of my room and to the door that I remembered from two days ago. Terrible memories flashed into my head, but I could do nothing about it. I flung open the door and started down the spinning stairs. When I got to the bottom I stood in front of the door to the loading dock.

As hard as I tried, I could not find a flashlight. But Robert did say that his men would have flashlights, so I was not going into this blind. I took a deep breath and opened the door. Unlike yesterday there was no naked bulb hanging above to give off light, they must have either shot it or turned it off.

I opened the door completely and stepped inside, darkness consuming me. Once the door was shutting to a close, with the brief ray of light I saw at least two pair of feet. Let's hope they are friendly. The door shut, and the metal frame provided a huge crash that seemed louder than normal.

I tried to look around the room, but it was near impossible. The darkness was everywhere, it felt like a being, not just how my eyes see. My fear was growing because of the fact that my eyes could not adjust. There was just no light at all for me to see.

"Hello?" I asked into the lightless environment.

"Over here." A voice said, around twenty feet in front of me. I started to walk over, placing my foot down as slowly as I could, fearing that I would trip and fall.

"It's OK; we cleaned the place out before this." A voice said right behind me.

"Right over here." The first voice said, and a burst of light was emitted from where the voice came. The man had turned on a flashlight.

I blinked several times for my eyes to adjust, and when they finally did, I hurried over to the man.

"Thanks," I said, taking the gun from him. It was like the gun that I had before in the cemetery, black. Where did I put that gun? I bet that it disappeared like the rest of the things that I had with me when I got transported to Paris. Then the man pointed the flashlight up to his face, like parents do when telling scary stories around the campfire.

"Now there is something that you need to remember," he said but then stopped. His gaze left me and looked up.

"HE'S A TRAITOR!" a voice behind me screamed into the darkness.

"I'm not a...," I started to say then realized the man wasn't talking about me. One of the men in the loading dock, most likely armed, was a traitor. This wasn't good.

I looked back up to the man in front of me. He briefly opened his mouth, and then got shot straight in the forehead. I shielded my eyes from the wave of blood and sticky pieces of skin that was flying at me. I quickly threw myself to the ground, along with the lit flashlight that dropped from the dead man's hands. I heard gunshots from all around me, and screamed. I grabbed the flashlight and pointed it toward where I heard the most gunshots.

My hands were shaky what I had just witnessed, so the flashlight's light was not steady. All that I got was a moving circle of light just briefly showing me a man shooting, then another man getting shot, blood bursting out.

Then I heard a shot from directly behind me, and the top of the flashlight exploded, sending metal and glass everywhere.

"Lights out!" I heard a raspy voice from behind me say. I was yet again thrust into darkness. Since my eyes had gotten accustomed to the light, this was shocking.

I rolled to the left as I heard another gunshot behind me, and a quick flash of light. The man behind me was trying to shoot at me, but could not see me. The only bad thing was I could not see him either.

I winced as I felt the ground rumble to the right of me as I avoided the shot. I thrust out my arm and smacked his leg as hard as possible as the gunshots continued behind me.

"NOW!" I heard a voice yell, and two bright lights were exposed behind me, hurting my eyes. The men behind me were most likely trying to disable their enemy's eyes, to confuse them. They waved the flashlights around, giving the loading dock various spotlights. I felt like I was at a night concert, lights flashing everywhere. But the shots continued.

I quickly jumped up, and when a light flashed my way, and I could see the rough face of the enemy, I shoved my fist to the man's face. I heard him scream and I ducked as he raised his gun, trying to see in the bizarre lights flashing around.

Someone yelled behind me, and one of the flashlights dropped to the ground, followed by a dead body. I turned as the man tried to find me and shoot me. When his gun illuminated by the light, I grabbed the top of the gun and tried to push it away. The man shot the gun twice, and both times I not only averted it, but felt the heat on my two hands that were holding onto it.

Finally I pulled the gun from the man's hands, and threw it to the ground. The man then tackled me. As the lights flashed everywhere, he punched my face once, twice, then three times. I felt like I was in a fun house at the carnival, the lights and fighting added a form of intensity and an adrenalin rush. I grabbed the man's hand when he tried to punch me a third time, and bent his fist back. He screamed and I kicked him back.

I grabbed the gun off the ground and once the light flashed over the man, I shot him twice. The lights continued to scatter everywhere, one revealing the guts that flew out of the back of the man's body. I started to crawl on my hands and knees, trying to avoid the bullets overhead. When the flashing lights told me that I had reached the door, the sounds behind showed that the fight behind me was not over. Would I really leave the people on my side behind?

I swore at my decision and stood up, aiming the gun in front of me. It seemed that the men on my side were flashing the lights and were on the right. The others were on the left. I quickly ran to the right side, not knowing if these were the good guys or not. I guess it depends if they shoot me or not when I join them.

I ran to the side of one of the two men, and pointed my gun at the others. He was waving a flashlight around, and it was better on this side of the light. I easily picked out a man on the other side and shot one bullet into his forehead, sending blood out like air out of punctured balloon. The man dropped.

"Good Job!" The man beside me yelled, and pointed the flashlight into my face.

"Dude, I can't see!" I screamed, fearing through my blindness that I would soon get a bullet in my face.

Then I realized that I had picked the wrong side. The men on the left were actually on my side, and now I was on the side of the traitors. I swore again and dropped to the ground, feeling a bullet graze my hair and briefly my skin, causing a minimal amount of blood. I fell to the hard concrete floor and quickly rolled to the side where the good guys were. I felt the ground rumble again as a bullet slammed into the ground. But that was it. The man was now waving his flashlight to the floor, trying to find me in the darkness.

He could not find me though because instead of rolling all the way to the other side, I had stopped after five feet or so. Now the man was confused, and with the flashlight pointed down, a small ray of light made it to his face, exposing him. I brought up my gun, and before I could shoot him, someone on the left side did it for me. The man's head exploded, blood flying. The corpse dropped the flashlight, and then dropped to the ground, sending a spatter of blood across the concrete.

When the flashlight rolled to me, I quickly flicked it off and rolled out of the way from where I once was. The last man standing on the bad side would be able to know where I was when I turned off the flashlight, so I moved. From the one waving flashlight, the men on the left could not see where the man was, they were shooting into pure darkness, then a quick flash of light, then repeat.

I slowly moved my way to the man on the right, crawling over to him. From my vantage point I could see his face just barely. When I was so close that I could touch him, I slowly stood up. I did not want him to hear me. When my face was level with his I could see the anger in his face, the blood-shot eyes. I lifted up the flashlight until it was pointed into the man's eyes, and turned it on.

The man screamed from surprise as the light shot into his eyes. Then I quickly flashed it off, sending him into darkness. He dropped his flashlight, and it shattered on the floor, sending everyone into darkness. I reached out my hand to punch the man, but all that I got was air. Where was he?

I skulked backward, carefully placing my steps.

"WHERE IS HE?!" One voice yelled. There was a quick burst of light and I heard a body fall to the ground. I kept walking backward until I felt the wall, and started walking around it. The key was to keep moving, quietly. I could not see, but he couldn't either. If I kept moving then at least I have some chance that if he shoots he will miss.

I had to keep quiet. The only reason that the other man was shot was because he had made a noise, attracting the bullet to his position. After the body slammed against the concrete, everything went silent. I tried to steady my breath, calm myself. But I was utterly afraid. Darkness was always something that I had hated from when I was a little boy, afraid from when my mom would turn off the lights for bedtime. I just wanted to quickly disappear into a nice dream, one where there was only light. And now not only did I have darkness, but a murdering sociopath. But was I really so different? How many people have I killed in the past month? Twenty, maybe less or more? What was wrong with me? People say that killing is hard. I guess that I've proved people wrong.

I stayed against the wall as I heard a gunshot, and a body slam to the ground. From the lack of an 'all clear' or something like that, I knew that it was just me, and the other man. He must be pretty smart for surviving this long in a dark environment.

"Come and get me, Melvin! You little piece of crap!" a rough voice called out. I raised my gun, pointing it to where the voice came from. But I did not dare shoot, because if I missed then the man would know where I was. I could feel my hands shaking, causing the gun to do the same. The man went from loud and obnoxious to being completely silent. I did not hear his feet step down, but I could sense that he was moving.

I silently continued my track along the wall, trying to keep my footsteps as quiet as possible by putting them down slowly. It was slowing me down, but it was the best that I could do. The gun was still pointed ahead, into the darkness. I felt like my hand was going out into a toxic cloud, the room felt like there was something there besides the man and me, something the consumed us all. It was the darkness. And it was scaring the skup out of me.

Then while I was thinking too much about the darkness, I made a mistake. I accidently kicked something with my foot, making a sound that echoed throughout the room. I was so screwed. Once I heard the first gunshot, I backpedaled a couple feet, being silent no longer my top priority. The bullet slammed into the wall that I was once using for a guide. Then I heard a second gunshot hit the concrete wall, and it must have shattered the concrete, because one piece slammed into my eye.

Acting upon instinct I quickly covered my eye, gun in hand. I took a couple of steps in random directions, trying to confuse the man while trying to get the piece of concrete out of my eye. When my eye was finally clear, I was surprised by the lack of gunshots. Everything was silent. The man must have lost my position. I reached out my hand to recover my wall that I used as a guide, but all I felt was air. I had moved around so much trying to get the concrete out of my eye that I had blindly wandered into the darkness. I was trapped in the man's game. He most likely knew exactly where I was, and was just messing with my head. I wanted to get to the door and get the hell out of here, but I could not. If I opened the door then light would flood in, telling my position. I just held where I was, closing my eyes, wishing it all to be over.

Then I felt warm fingers breeze through my hair and a raspy voice behind me.

"Nice hair. Blonde is it?" I heard behind me. I quickly flung out my arm to strike him, but I met nothing but darkness. He moved too quickly.

"You freaking coward! Stop moving." I yelled out of pure fear, my voice cracking. I really hate the darkness.

"I can hear the fear in your voice. Afraid of the dark?" The voice said.

"Get the hell away from me." I said quietly.

"What was that? I could not hear you over the pure fear you were emitting." The man said, I could even hear his smile.

"GET THE SKUP AWAY FROM ME!" I yelled, lashing out with my right fist. Again, I was greeted with nothing. Where was he!

"I felt some wind there!" The man said, mocking me.

"Skup you,"

"No man, skup you." He said, and I felt the cold metal of a gun being pushed into my skull. He was going to kill me at point blank.

"Come on, do you really want to shoot me at point blank?" I said, trying to distract him.

"Why not?" He asked.

"I'll tell you why not. Because all the blood and whatever else that skupping comes out of my head will cover you. How will you be able to leave the building without attracting attention?" I said, smiling. The man pondered this, not speaking.

"What the hell is that suppose to mean?" He said but before he could swear again I jabbed back my elbow, hitting him in the stomach. He tried to raise his gun to shoot me, but couldn't because I had knocked the breath out of him. I then turned around quickly and blindly lashed out my fist, striking what I thought was his mouth. He gasped in and I felt around for his neck.

When I finally got it I threw him to the ground, and randomly brought my foot down, hoping to hit him in the darkness. I felt my foot collide with him a couple of times. That is what he got for being a total freak. I then lashed out my foot one more time, and upon hitting him, pointed my gun to where I kicked him.

Then I shot the gun twice, and everything went silent. I had most likely hit him. After that I turned to where I thought the door was and started walking, hands out in front. When I finally hit the wall I felt for a light switch. I guess that I was becoming more accustomed to the darkness, I was still scared, but now I was less scared. I had realized that it was less scary when there was not someone trying to kill you inside the darkness.

I found the light switch in the dark and flicked it on. A single hanging light bulb was hanging from the ceiling, and it covered the place with light. I blinked my eyes to adjust to the light, and when I was finally adjusted I took a look around.

The first thing I saw was blood splatter everywhere. It was on the floor, the walls, even a little bit on the ceiling. Most blood splatters were next to a body, but some were as much as ten feet away, signaling that the bullet had gone through the body, and smashed into a wall, taking the blood with it.

Then I noticed the bodies. Most had bullet holes in the head, blood slowly seeping out. One man's eye had been shot, revealing a hole full of blood and sticky pieces of whatever is in an eye. I stepped over that body and found the man that I had the final showdown with. I had shot him twice in the chest; pieces of guts were now hanging out. Pieces of metal were scattered on the ground from the broken flashlights. I bet that Robert did not plan for me to be the only survivor.

What had I gotten myself into? There were five dead bodies on the ground. Five souls that were now gone from this world, gone forever. Did I really deserve to live while these people died? What makes me more special than them?

This life was not my life to live. I had cheated with my life, fast-forwarding through the years. I knew how this was going to end. I knew that the world would be taken over by the people that once promised to be "green". The people that once built skyscrapers and tore down forests and killed thousands of animals would now take it all back. Once everyone got turned into demons except for the lucky survivors, there would be no one to care for the giant buildings. They will crumble to the ground eventually with no one to care for them. Vegetation will take over. The plants and everything, the trees and plants, everything, will return to where they were supposed to be. What if I let this happen? We humans have been so terrible to this world, and once we all go crazy, then the world would return to what it was supposed to be.

Humans or vegetation? If I save the humans, then we will continue to let bad things happen to the environment. But if I don't.........Wait, what the skup was I thinking? If I save the humans, it's not like every skupping tree will explode. We are trying our hardest to save everything. We are so close to having a "green" world, and I would not want to spoil it now.

I walked out of the loading dock, ready for all the action for today. I reminded myself that all the action that just went on will be multiplied. I guess that the whole "darkness battle" had warmed me up for today. It was basically me verses an entire army of terrorists. I will not only have to deal with the man that I faced on the Eiffel Tower a couple of days ago, but I will also have to deal with his backup. This was nuts. How could I survive? What if I didn't? What would happen if I died? Would Robert then come in with his group? Why didn't his group come with me in the first place? Why did they have to leave it all to me?

And why me anyway? Why did they pick me and not some random French guy? Was it because of my secret? Did they even know it? I thought that only a couple people in the government knew about it, and the police. I was very lucky for not going to jail after what I did, and I will always be sorry for what happened. It was a big mistake, what I did. I never meant to hurt anyone; I just wanted to protect myself. And then I promised to never use the device again, and here I was, with parts of it in my closet in the room.

I walked up the stairs, through the hallway and then to my hotel room. I had to get ready for the battle today. I had taken another handgun from one of the dead men, so now I had three, all looking the same. I put one in each pocket, and put the parts of the device in my back pocket. I never knew when I would need them. The third gun I had no idea what to do with. I put on a light coat that I bought, and stuck the third gun into my pocket. It's game time.

Just then the cell phone rang, and I flicked it open.

"You need to go NOW." Robert said quickly.

"No time to rest?" I asked.

"No, the bombing will happen in around twenty minutes." He responded.

"Why didn't you call me earlier?" I said, not mentioning that I was already dressed and ready to go.

"I heard there was a battle in the loading dock. I had men listening to what was happening from outside." He said.

"And they didn't feel the need to help?"

"OK, you need to go now. DO NOT get a taxi. You do not know how bad traffic will be, you may never get there."

"OK, next time we talk; it'll be in a demon-free world." I said and hung up. The butterflies in my stomach started to sprint now, expanding my jitters.

Chapter 10

It was time. Time to save, or destroy the world. All my life it has come to this. To either save, or destroy. There is a time in every man's life where he must either do one or the other. This was my chance to step up.

I had to get the Eiffel Tower early, to save time. I sprinted towards the hall, closed the door, and ran to the stairs. I ran in circles down the metal-grated stairs, getting dizzy by the time I had reached the bottom, pushing open the door marked "LOBBY". Once there I made my way through the large room, passing all types or tourists. They will see their home again. They will not die here. I forbid it.

Once outside I took a deep breath. It was time. I scanned the horizon and found the entrance for the park "Jardin des Tuileries". If I go straight through that park, it should lead me to the Eiffel Tower.

I ran across the street, not caring about pushing people aside. Once I made it to the park entrance, I took a quick look at the large tourist map. I was right; it was not a long way to the Eiffel Tower. I started to run through the park, my green coat zippered to avoid the gun being seen. I passed various statues and fountains, running on the pebble road that runs straight through the park. On both sides there were trees, and behind them, benches for people to sit and read, or just plain relax.

I ran through, not stopping. There were dark clouds in the skies, threatening rain. The wind was beginning to blow in gusts, causing the flowers to move like fans at a Muse concert. I saw the wind blow off one man's hat, and he ran after it. I felt my black-dyed-blonde head felt the chill of the wind. It was around fifty-seven degrees out; almost everyone was wearing a coat. But the chill helped me run. I remember when I was on the cross-country team at my school, everything was running.

This helped me now as I remembered the one thing that always kept me going. My coach would always let us know that if we feel like we should stop, we NEED to do the exact opposite. Stopping was out of the question. If you are sick, run to the hospital.

Whenever I started to get hot in the coat, a breeze of wind would cool me down. It helped me through everything. This day was perfect for a final battle, everything about it just screamed "intense". The wind, the clouds, everything. As I ran past the various kinds of trees, the first raindrop fell, landing on my head. This added to the intensity, a dream for everything. A final battle should not be on a sunny day, but a day like today.

Dark clouds threatened to crush me from above, with a grey outline and middle as black as a pupil. Then the drops fell harder, turning into a shower. My fleece coat was wet and starting to get colder and maybe eventually freeze. I stopped by a trash can and tore off my coat, took out the gun, and threw the coat into the trash. It was ruined from the rain. I squeezed the gun into my right pocket with the other one, and shivered in the cold weather. All that I had on was my Muse t-shirt, nothing more on my upper-body.

I turned and saw something of interest. The man from the Eiffel Tower. He even had the backpack on. I stared at him, trying to make sure it was really him without losing time. He was under a tree, on the phone trying not to get wet. Middle-aged, balding, and skinny, yes that was him. He looked behind him and our eyes met. He saw the gun in my hand and said something quick into the phone then shut it, and jammed it into his pocket. Then from his other pocket he took out a handgun like mine.

I dove behind the trash can as I felt two bullets breeze by me. I looked over the trash can; the man had taken cover behind a tree. I saw him aim with his gun, and I tucked my head down onto my legs. A bullet slammed into the metal trash can, making it shake. I turned my entire body to the left, and looked around the left side of the can. I then shot once, bullet slamming into the tree. Once I was done I moved back to my cover behind the can. I felt another bullet go into the can.

Behind me I could hear police sirens from behind the carnival in the park. Scared mothers picked up their children and got the hell out of the park. I saw the people who were once on the benches reading now screaming and running for their lives.

I looked over the can. The man was trying to reload, hiding himself behind the tree. I used this opportunity to note the tree to my left, my back to the trash can. I quickly ran to the tree to get behind it, where I at least was able to stand up straight. The top of the tree was blocking the rain, only a couple of drops would get by the wall of leaves.

I heard the man yell as he shot two new bullets into the trash can. I could see the confused look as he realized that I was not there anymore. I looked over the left side of the tree, brought my arm around, and shot twice at him. I hit the tree, missing the man.

He finally realized where I was and shot a bullet at me. I took cover behind the tree, and the bullet sent bark flying. I listened for the police sirens, but they seemed to be gone. All that I heard was gunfire. Was the man still shooting at me? I looked in front of the tree and did not see the man behind the tree. I looked to the pebbles on the ground and saw his shadow, it was there. He was still behind the tree.

As the rain poured down, I looked beyond the tree to where I first came from, the entrance to the park. I saw a couple police cars parked out in front, and officers hiding behind the car. What were they hiding from? I looked further and saw two men shooting at the police officers. No doubt they were part of the man's crew. Robert Bellamy said that he would have help with him.

I turned back to the man and shot two bullets at him. I heard him cry out, did I hit him? I did not want to look; I would be making myself a target. Instead I stood still, hiding behind the tree, appreciating the cover.

Then I heard one bullet whiz by me, and it was close, it was not against the police officers. I looked to my right; the man had shot an old woman in the arm, blood pouring out. I wanted to go help her. But if I did, I would totally lose my cover, and he would shoot me. I heard the man chuckle as I had to make my decision. The rain continued to pour down, adding to the old woman's tears. She cried out for help. I saw a teenage boy run over to try to help her; I heard a shot and the boy's head erupted in blood. He fell to the ground, dead. The blood was freely flowing onto the ground around the boy.

No more killing for this man. I looked around the right side of the tree and shot a bullet at him, and it glazed his arm, sending a piece of his coat flying. He was thrown off by surprise, and I leaned over to the left side of the tree and shot a bullet to the left side, just missing his exposed neck. He was throwing himself to the right, trying to shield himself.

I heard an ambulance in the background. Good, at least one French person was not stupid enough to walk into the battlefield to try to help someone. Better to call on the professionals to help. But it was also bad news, it means that the paramedics would have to get into the battlefield to save the woman, and they will probably bring armed backup. Their backup does not know that I am a good guy; I'm just another person with a gun.

I knew that the man had noticed this, because he just decided to run. He ran to the right of the rows of trees, exposed to the rain. When I heard the pebbles crunching and the splashing of puddles, I knew I had to run to catch up. The backpack was bobbing up and down, and so was his head. I brought up the gun, but could not get a clean shot. I pulled the trigger just in case I got lucky, and was greeted with a clicking sound. I was all out of ammo.

I ran past a fountain with three holes spurting out water, with a statue of a man with three heads above it. When I ran past it, I threw the empty gun into the water, making a small splash. Then I continued to run after my opponent, shortening the distance between us. The gunshots behind me were joined by screams, and sounds of people dying. I kept running forward, I could not let anything distract me.

As I ran, I realized that despite the pouring down rain, I had a perfect shot at the man. I could have taken out another gun to shoot the man, but it would slow me down. I sprinted to keep up, and even with the backpack the man was fast. I should have known from his body type that he was going to be fast. He most likely exercises all the time. And then there was me, who is not used to these conditions of chill, rain, and wind.

The sweat running down my face was the proof that I was running hard, the wind making hard resistance. I hoped that once we got to the Eiffel Tower I would be close enough to tackle him to the ground and bring an end to this madness. I would not get the help from the police; they will all be trying to give their comrades help at the entrance to the park. I was on my own.

Then my mind flashed back to about five minutes ago, when I was looking at the map. I had seen that right after the park was a five lane road, and behind it was the Eiffel Tower. The man will not stop for a red light because he knew that I would catch him. He would continue running, putting his and my life in danger. Cars go fast here in Paris, and the taxi cab drivers are crazy.

I sprinted, losing my breath, trying to steady it. I had not run cross-country in at least five years. Ultimate Frisbee had helped me stay active, but I was only trained for the short sprints, not long runs ones like this. And I was definitely not used to these conditions. Sure, we played in the rain, but not strong winds that knock hats off of people and blow umbrellas inside out.

I ran and ran, losing my perseverance. I felt my lungs begin to spasm, yelling at me for performing this crazy stunt. I felt like I was going to die, have a heart attack. My palms started to get all sweaty and my forehead as well. Sweat started to get in my eyes, impacting my vision. I quickly wiped my eyes, keeping them on the man. I tried to remember how long this park was. One mile? Half a mile? Two miles?

I continued to run, not letting the pain bring me down. I had a world to save, and this man had a world to destroy. It was time for us face fist to fist. But that would only happen if I caught up. This would never happen if I stopped to take a breath or loss my focus.

Robert Bellamy never said how difficult this was going to be. I guess that I never really expected a road race. All that I thought that I would have to do is take a taxi to the Eiffel Tower, point out the man and yell bomb, and then get a medal for bravery. Then go back to America a hero. Now already one child has died. And I do not know how many police officers had died so far.

Then the man in front of me passed by an elderly man taking a walk and grabbed him by the neck and held him in a choke hold. The punk was taking a hostage.

"STOP THIS MADNESS!" I yelled.

"SKUP YOU!" he yelled, holding the gun pointed to the man's head.

"CAN'T YOU JUST SEE THAT IT IS OVER? I'M HERE! THE POLICE NOW KNOW THAT YOU ARE THREATENING TO BOMB THE EIFFEL TOWER!" I screamed.

"THEY CAN'T STOP ME! NO ONE CAN!" he screamed back, rain dropping down.

"DO YOU EVEN KNOW WHAT WILL HAPPEN ONCE YOU BOMB IT!!!!? THE WHOLE WORLD WILL BE THROWN INTO CHAOS!!!!!" I yelled.

"ISN'T THAT WHAT IS SUPPOSE TO HAPPEN WHEN YOU EXPLODE A BOMB!" he said, mocking me. The hostage he took was keeping quiet -- smart man.

"YOU DON'T UNDERSTAND! YOU NEVER WILL! NOW JUST LET THE MAN GO!" I yelled.

"SKUPPING NEVER!" he said.

"THEN WE'LL JUST STAY HERE, GUNS POINTED AT ONE ANOTHER, UNTIL THE POLICE COME AND THEN IT WILL BE OVER!" I yelled. I could see in his face that he understood me.

"SKUP!!!!!!!!!!" He yelled and pushed the man to the ground, his head hitting against the pebbles and landing in a puddle. The man continued on his sprint. I swore, realizing that I could have taken out my gun, but now it was too late, I had to try to catch up with him.

I could hear the cars before I saw them. The honking and tires against wet concrete were everywhere, disturbing the park.   I ran we passed by The Louve, which housed the Mona Lisa and other great pieces of artwork. I wish that I had gotten a chance to look inside, see everything. I could see the crowd lining up out front wanting to go inside as much as I did. I thought I saw a couple familiar faces, but who the hell did I know in Paris? Was one of them Robert Bellamy? I would never know because I had to keep running, I had to catch up with the man.

Then once we started up a hill, I had to kick it into high gear. This is where I would either catch up to him, or lose him forever. If he started to slow down on this hill, I could catch up to him and take him down before he even got to the Eiffel Tower. But he seemed to be used to hills, he ran up it like it was nothing. I had to catch up to him! I just had to, to save to the world!

I looked down at the pebbles and the water running down the hill and pushed myself, running up the hill to gain speed. I kept the thoughts of me losing out of my head, and tried to keep them there forever. There was a way to change the future. And that way was me catching up to bomber.

When I made it up the hill there was a flat ground of maybe thirty yards before the road. The road scared me like a screaming banshee. It scared me like the dark, it was so intimidating, so big and grand.

Five lanes of speeding cars that would not stop for anything. And beyond that was the Eiffel Tower, it reached up and was taller than anything else. All of the buildings were so small compared to it, like a toy army man to the actual man in uniform. Most of the buildings were made out of white brick, adding a renaissance look to the horizon. Then I was reminded of the battle at hand. All these buildings would be destroyed come the apocalypse that I was trying to prevent.

Then I saw the man continue to run, not even thinking about waiting for the red light. I thought about how scary this would be, not counting on how dangerous it was going to be. My life was hanging by a thread already. I did not need speeding cars to add to my problems. But you know what? Skup it, I needed to save the world.

The man ran into the road, cars honking. I ran after him. Once my feet left the sidewalk my safety left too. I ran through, cars honking at me, demanding that I stop. But I continued to run; I needed to catch up with the evil man. I heard a big crash behind me, metal crunching against one another, and the sequel of brakes of behind the collision trying to avoid it. People screamed and yelled at us. But I kept running, keeping my eye on the prize.

I saw a car stop ahead of me and the man jump over its hood. He just skimmed the top, and within seconds he was back on his feet running on the concrete. I went to do the same but another car slammed into the back of the first, causing metal to fly. A black car pushed a white truck forward, blocking my path. I made a quick decision and dove under the white truck, slamming into the pavement then quickly rolling under the truck, the smell of oil and metal entering my nose. I continued rolling, hoping the truck would not move forward and crush me.

When I could once again see the sky, I got up and continued running, not even taking time to brush off all the dirt on me. I saw the man ahead of me, about to dodge a car. But the hood of the car slammed into the man, causing him to fall to the ground. I wondered why it had taken three lanes for one of us to finally be hit.

Now that he was on the ground, I was sure I to catch up to him. I sprinted ahead as he got up and tried to run some more. I saw his hand on his hip, he most likely got scratched or something. I had to use this to my advantage.

I ran past the car that hit the man, the driver now leaning out the window yelling in French. The man was running again, but looked hurt.

Another car almost hit the man in, but stopped at the last second, the driver not completely engaged in his texting. Even though the car did not hit him, the man still stuck out his hand to protect himself, and stopped. I used this to my advantage, sprinting up to the stopped man who was just realizing that he could start running again. I jumped through the air, taking the man down with me. We bumped together, and we fell to the ground, smashing against the car as we went.

I was on top of him, and I did not want to ruin this opportunity, I did not want to lose my position. Right now I had the upper hand. If I lost it, he would kill me for sure. I struck out my fist, smashing it into his forehead, surely giving him a headache. He lashed out with his arm, and I quickly grabbed it and pushed it back down to the pavement. He tried with his left arm then, and I pushed it down with my left arm. I had him pinned.

He continued to try to move around, to get out of the hold that I had him in. Cars honked all around, demanding us to move but yet too cowardly to get the skup out of their cars to help. Every time the man would lift one arm up, I would slam it back to where it belonged, the cement.

Then the man did something that I could have never anticipated. He quickly lifted up his head, bashing it into mine. Out of pure surprise I lifted my hands off of his arms for a brief second, and he used that chance to slam his hands into my chest, pushing me back. When I was high enough off of the ground and away from him he lashed out his foot, hitting me in the stomach.

I lost my air right away, everything in my lungs now gone. I fell to the left, my upper body hitting the ground. The man started to stand up, then saw my hanging head and lashed out with his fist. His fist hit my ear, and I tried to recover, but I was still recovering from the blow to my stomach. I tried to scream as the man stood up, and shoved his foot into my face, causing me to fall down the ground.

He brought down his foot into my face as I started to regain my breath. He smashed his foot against my head twice more before turning to yell at one of the drivers. I started to slowly get up, and he swore and lashed out with his foot again. It hit my cheek and I saw a flash of red, he had cut me with his shoe. I screamed out in pain. He then got on his knee next to me.

"I'm going to take you out! You can't stop what I'm going to do!" he whispered into my ear, and I was too hurt to move.

"And how did that work out last time?" I mocked him, my cheek hurting when I moved it.

"I don't know how the hell you survived, I skupping threw you off the Eiffel Tower!" he yelled. My strength was slowly growing, attack plans swirling around in my head.

"Well maybe next time, you won't throw me on top of an elevator." I said, smiling just a little.

Before the man could say anything I threw out my right fist, smacking him in the jaw. He fell back, and I brought up my right foot into his chest, knocking him down to the ground. I punched him once more before starting to stand up, first getting onto my knees. But he was quick to recover; he moved his leg off of the ground and kicked out to my face, striking the top of my nose. My head turned to the side, trying to avoid the next blow but he grabbed my head and smashed my face to the ground.

Before my head hit the pavement, I quickly closed my eyes. As my forehead bumped into the cement rather violently, and when he lifted my head back up I saw a bit of blood on the ground. He then smashed my head into the cement once more, and when he pulled me back up I could see the blood filling the cracks of the cement, a lot of blood. I would have brought up my hand to see how big the cut was, but before I could I met the ground again. I felt the place on my forehead where it was sore, and I felt warm sticky blood washing down my face.

The man then stuck his knee into my back, causing me to cry out. My head almost dropped to the ground, but I pushed back, and I did not feel the man's hands behind my head to push me down again. Why was he not pushing me into the ground again? I got my answer when something big and hard smashed into my head, causing me to see stars. He had grabbed a rock and was now banging it into my head. I had to get him off of me, but I could not move with his knee jabbing into my spine.

He hit me a couple more times; I felt warm sticky blood running down the back of my neck. Then the stream of blood made its way down my forehead, over my nose, avoiding my eyes, and went straight in to my mouth. I tasted iron inside my mouth as he smashed my head again. The pulsing of the top of my head did not help the headache that was slowly growing, going into the nerves deep within my head and tugging at them with all its might.

I realized that with him banging the rock into my skull with his right hand meant that my right arm was free; I could do whatever I wanted with it. I could not hit him, my arm was bent forwards and I could not bend it back enough to smack him. And if I even tried it would take time, and he would notice me in that time. And then he would pull my arm back, maybe he would even break it.

I did not care about what would happen, I flung back my arm as far as I could, and I felt it smack into his fist holding the rock. He yelled out and grabbed that arm with both hands, leaving my left arm free. I took that opportunity and flung out my left arm, pushing it against his body, and pushed him over, making him face the ground. We were now reversing positions. I had used my left arm as leverage, making him fall by pushing him backwards.

As he fell to the ground, I turned around to face him, we both on the ground in front of the car. I punched him in the nose, making him taste sweet revenge. I then made my fist taste his forehead, causing him to grunt and look away. I grabbed the two sides of his forehead with my two index fingers and turned his head toward me. He smiled much to my confusion.

The man flung his foot forward, kicking me in the chest, and he kept his leg extended, pushing me back. My fingers left his forehead, and with his foot pushing me back he flung out his fist, striking me in the eye. I screamed and he pushed my face back, while my hands went to my eye to recover. It was stinging like a bee as the man slowly got up.

"I told you. No skupping stopping me." He said and started to walk away, realizing I was no longer a threat. I continued to lie down, just thinking to myself how easy I was to defeat. The cars honked at him, and I watched through one eye as he ignored everything and kept walking, finally getting to the other side of the road, walking on the sidewalk now, backpack with bomb inside still on his back.

Once my eye quit screaming, I slowly got back up to my feet. Once I was completely up, I scanned the area. At least three cars collided, everyone yelling at one another in French. The man in the white truck was yelling at another man next to him, distracted as I walked past. I walked with no intention of running to catch up with the man as he walked. My leg was hurting, so I had a slight limp. I knew that once I continued to walk on it the hurt would go away and I would be back to normal. My eye still bit at my nerves, and a slight pulse had found a home under it. My knees were covered in dust and blood, pretty much destroying the jeans that I was wearing.

I lifted my head, no longer looking at my knees and saw that the man was trying to disappear in the crowd, moving away from me, toward the looming Eiffel Tower in the distance. At least I knew where he was going, but he would most likely set up the bomb right when he got there, and then make a break for it. He would most likely hide the bomb somewhere so that I cannot find it, and then set it off from a distance, with some kind of remote control. I cannot just listen for a ticking sound, it is not that easy.

Bombs these days could look like anything. If the government has the power to make me skupping travel through time I think that terrorists can at least hide a bomb. Technology was so bad; things could happen that we thought could never happen. But yet it is sneaking up on humanity like a skupping snake in the grass.

I walked onto the sidewalk, getting closer and closer to the Eiffel Tower. It was looming, unlike anything that I have ever seen in my life. Pictures and videos underestimate it; it was much more majestic in person. I loved it; I could not see how anyone could dislike it. It was a masterpiece. A masterpiece that would be soon destroyed if I did not do anything about it.

I walked up, ready at any time to take the gun out of my right pocket. But as I walked, I could not see him at all in the crowd. The Eiffel Tower seemed to grow bigger as I got closer, escaping from my line of vision. The top was slowly disappearing, as well as the thin stack of metal at the top. I kept my eyes to the crowd, looking around for mystery man. I tried also looking at the back of everyone, looking for the colorful backpack.

As I walked farther forward, the mass of people grew. I felt like I was walking slowly into a toxic wade of air, everything was getting tight. I went from having one person at least two feet away to touching everyone at the shoulders. My limp was gone, replaced by a fast moving leg. I started to pick up the pace, trying my hardest to find him. Then my mind scared me, making me wonder if he was a suicide bomber. In that case he would not even stop to set up the bomb, he would just have to press a button and explode into a mass of blood and guts. In that case I had no time to lose, none at all. He could be picking out his spot next to a leg of the Tower right now, and I was too far away.

I started to jog through the crowd now, and I was under the Tower, where everyone was pushing as much as they could. My eyes were franticly looking around, trying to find the man, and feeling the guilt that if I don't find him the destruction of this world would be all on me. I looked everywhere, every voice that I hear tricking my ears into to thinking the man was close by. The wind blew all around me, and the brown metal of the Eiffel Tower tried to block the rain the best that it could, but some drops still got through. It did block my sight of the dark clouds forming above, but the intensity was still there.

I most likely looked horrible, dried blood looking like streaking my face, dirt and dust in my hair. My eyes were everywhere, and then once I thought that I would see his backpack or even his balding head or big muscles, it would end up being an illusion. I was so skupped if I did not find him. I pictured the back right leg of the "Tower" exploding, sending people and blood flying, and if that did not kill me then the falling metal would. All of the people standing on the observation decks would fall too, smashing their heads on the hard cement below, sending red goo everywhere that the wind blew.

I tried not to think about it as I looked. Everything seemed to go in slow motion, the butterflies in my stomach expanding to monsters. Tears started to fill my eyes. All was lost. I had lost him, and now everyone would lose their lives, thanks to me. I tried to push the thought away, but it stayed there like an ignorant punk. I looked and looked, but my eyes could not find him.

I looked to the left and right, but someone would walk by and push me to the side, looking into their camera or cell phone screen. Sometimes they would say "sorry" in whatever skupping language they spoke and continue walking. I looked everywhere that I could, even jump over the crowd to see if my eyes could spot that backpack. It was not that big of an area under the Tower, I should be able to see him! But why couldn't I? Where was he?

I quickly grabbed a woman in the crowd that looked English. She was wearing a red raincoat and big sunglasses.

"Have you seen a muscle-ly man with a crazy backpack on? With balding hair!" I asked franticly.

"Nope, believe me, I have been looking for one of those all my life." She laughed and continued walking.

My heart was beating faster than it ever should. It felt like an animal inside of my chest, pounding to get out. The tears stopped, and the fear grew to a huge unbearable level. I felt like I was a father who had lost his child in the crowd, and was now too cocky to ask a security agent to help. I needed to find the bomber if it was the last thing that I ever did, which it could very well be. Once I find him, what will stop him from shooting my head off? Either way, I was not going to give up. No skupping way that was ever happening.

I ran my fingers through my short hair, trying to ease the fear pulsing deep through my veins, making me slowly go insane. I looked everywhere, starting with the right leg farthest away from me, then to the left leg farthest away, then back to the closer left leg, and finally to the closer right leg, then to the middle of the mass of people everywhere. I could not see the man in the group, nor could I ever hope to. If I had not left the cell phone back in my room, I would call Robert Bellamy and told him that I need more time. Make him give me a chance to travel through time again, and this time make things right.

Then once I thought all was lost, out of the corner of my eye, I saw the backpack. My heart fluttered as I turned my entire head to see. It was him. He was standing outside from underneath the Eiffel Tower, next to the left leg farthest away from me. He was sitting at a café table, resting on a chair and the backpack on the table. Why was he just sitting down? Why wasn't he trying to activate the bomb, make us all go boom?

I started to make my way through the crowd, to under the Tower, away from the cover. I used my elbows and pushed people away, my mind racing. Why was the backpack just sitting there? Was he sitting at the café to get a drink? Was the plan destroyed? Did the good guys win? The leader assassinated? What the skup, why was he not doing anything?

As I walked out from under the Tower, the rainfall started to get heavier, the wet blobs dropping onto my head. The man looked happy sitting under a purple umbrella, with a cup of hot liquid in his hands. Right after I left the relative cover of the brown metal above me, the crowds started to get smaller. I no longer had a right and left hand man or woman; everyone was at least five feet away on all sides. There were giant flat rocks everywhere for children to climb on, but mostly to the side where trees were in lines. People walked over to concession stands and got popcorn or drinks, some buying rain coats and umbrellas. It was another normal day for the workers at the Eiffel Tower, working all day on the hard concrete ground.

When I got close to the man, I knew that I had to take him out, threat or not. I hid behind one of the big trees before the café, around twenty feet or so from the man. He seemed to have not noticed me yet, and seemed comfortable in his metal chair and the warming drink in his hand. I looked around to make sure no eyes were on me, and then went to grab the gun from my right pocket of my jeans.

When I pulled the handle of the gun, it would not come out. I tugged some more, and still it stayed. It must be stuck on a thread deep inside the pocket of the jeans. I reached my hands down into the pocket, and felt the top of the gun. I was right; a bit of the top was stuck on a thread. I looped the thread off of the top, and went to take the gun out. But when I started to lift my hand out of the pocket to close it around the handle to take it out, I felt a piece of paper.

Under the cover of the giant tree, I thought it was safe enough to take the paper out without it being ruined by the falling rain. I took it out, leaving the gun inside my pocket. The paper was one of those yellow lines ones that you find on notepads in offices. What was this doing in my pocket? I unfolded it slowly, ready to read what it had to say. It was written in pen, with uneducated cursive, although I could still read it.

To Whoever Finds This,

You know me as Chris. As a simple traveler in the apocalypse, I have a lot of secrets that I would wish to expose. Before I begin, you are probably wondering why I did not just tell you these secrets instead of using my pick pocketing skills to put this in your pocket before you notice what is going on. The answer is: I am ashamed. Embarrassed about what went on in the days before the world went demon-controlled. This may be a silly reason; but also, who can you trust when everything has gone bad? Who is even sane anymore? This is what went on in those days, the days when crazy people wearing suits and ties thought that setting off a bomb at the Louve was a good idea.

I should not get too ahead of myself. I work for a company, for legal reasons I will only say the 'Company'. We were not officially a terrorist group, but we did have a secret agenda besides our usual work of advertisement. We wanted the world to pay for what they had done, and for a while I was in on it as much as they were. I do not know why I was; I was born an American and loved my country and this world. But the Company gave me work; for most of the time I tried to stay away from their terrorist plans.

But when they started actually building the bomb, I started to get afraid. These guys were actually going to do it! At first I pretended to go along with it, but when a couple scientists of ours said that the bomb was unsafe, that its high levels of radioactive material could very well have uncharted effects on humans, I started to want to back out. I tried to quit, but they would not let me go. I had to stay and obey my boss, a man by the name of Robert Bellamy, who was a terrible man. He was the one who came up with the idea of destroying the Louve with a new radioactive bomb.

He knew that somehow the story would get out that the Company would do something bad, so he made up the story of a terrorist group trying to bomb the Eiffel Tower. He had one man, the one that he called 'Subject Zero'. He said that he told Subject Zero about all the bad things that would happen, and even transported him to the future to see the effects. Now, what Robert did not know was how uncontrolled it would be in the future. And even if he did, it would not matter. He wanted to kill everyone for what they had done to this world.

As the date came closer, and Robert assigned jobs to people, (fake bombers to go to the Eiffel Tower, stuff like that) more and more staff members began to drop out. Robert would just call them cowards and continue assigning, then sending his men to assassinate the 'traitors'. I kept my head down and nodded to everything, I did not want to die. But when *no one wanted to be the one to explode the bomb next to the Louve, in the little underground marketplace next to the entrance to the acclaimed palace of art, he nominated himself.*

I watched from a distance as he blew himself up, and was surprised when I did not see his guts fly everywhere. It must be a radioactive effect, I thought. But then the smoke cleared and I saw the anger in his eyes, he was not the same person. And when he ripped apart the woman who was running, I knew that the radioactive levels had turned him into some kind of monster, like a demon. I had to get away.

And it went from there. Now, three years after, I finally have the courage to write this down. I do not know how the curse of the demon spread to America and everywhere else, but now I hear that the entire world is destroyed. When Robert turned into the first demon, he was a lot more powerful than any of the demons here and now, most likely because of the lack of radiation. I feel relieved that I had the chance to put this all down on paper, to expose everything that has gone on.

With Hope for a New World, Chris

Chapter 11

I tried to control all of the thoughts running through my head. This was a major game-changer. Everything that I thought, everything that I knew, was all a lie. Robert Bellamy was behind it all. He tricked me into thinking that a terrorist group was going to bomb the Eiffel Tower, while he bombed the Louve behind my back! I was Subject Zero! That piece of skup!

But what if this was not true. But what motive could Chris have to lie to me? The world was already destroyed when he wrote this! But there was only one way to find out.

I took the gun out of my pocket and ran to the man sitting down with the backpack on the table.

"Is this true!" I yelled, gun pointed to his face. I held out the note and watched as the man silently read it.

"Please don't kill me! It was all Robert's idea! He volunteered to do the suicide bombing, and we all said OK! Please, I was not even thinking about bombing the Eiffel Tower! The backpack just has a box of shoes in it, no bomb!" he said quickly.

"Tell me where and when the bombing will happen, and I will spare your life." I said.

"You know the little marketplace underground? The one where the center is under the big glass triangle? Ya, that's where. Robert planned on going directly under the triangle and pushing the button, exploding everything." He said.

"When! When is this going to happen!" I yelled, feeling the pressure of the clock ticking away. The man lifted his arm out of his long sleeve shirt as I shivered in my t-shirt. The man frowned.

"You have ten minutes before the bombing. You better get a move on." The man said with concern in his eyes.

"SKUP!" I yelled, taking the gun away from the man's head. I had to move. I turned from the man, and way in the distance I could see the Louve, a small building. It would take me around fifteen minutes to get there by foot. A taxi would be too risky with all the traffic. I had to sprint, and sprint all the way. I held the gun in my right hand, knowing that people tend to get out of the way of people with guns.

"Please stop him," The man said as I started to run.

"Oh, don't worry. I will deal with him if it's the last thing I do." I said as I sprinted away, trying to pace myself. This was horrible. I had to hurry as fast as I could.

I ran around the underneath of the Tower, I did not want the giant crowds to hold me back. The raindrops hit my face and bare arms like knifes, but I knew that I had to keep moving. I was so skupped if I did not get there in time. But if worse came to worse, I still had the items that I bought at the electronics store. But I had to get him before he set off the bomb. The note said that the fist demon was a lot worse than the ones that I faced, so this was going to be difficult. What would I do if I am faced with the demon Robert Bellamy? Shoot him? I hardly think that will work.

Multiple people screamed and got out of the way as I ran with my gun in hand. I ran down the giant fifty-feet-across pebble walkway, leading straight for the Louve. It ended straight at the entrance to go underground, under the big glass triangle that acted like a window for the people underground to see above. There were tons of little shops down there, then a ticket window and finally the stairs into the Louve. I could picture Robert standing there right under the triangle, waiting to push the button, making peace with whatever skupped-up god he worships.

This reminded me of all the final stretches that I have done in my days of cross-country. Once you get going, you cannot stop until you reach the finish, and that was my plan. My breath was going fast, my heart beating faster. The butterflies were completely gone in my stomach, nothing there except for confidence and hope. I could do this! This was my one chance to change the world. I would be a hero, something that everyone wants to be. A little boy, jumping off the couch with a bed sheet tied around his neck, proclaiming that he is superman. Now that little boy was sprinting through Paris, rain all around, wind providing resistance. This was the chance we all want. And there was no skupping way that I was going to mess it up.

How much time has passed? At least seven minutes, maybe more. I had limited time. I stopped about twenty feet away from the giant glass triangle rising out of the ground. I took a quick look behind me at the Eiffel Tower, giving myself a little fist pump for making it this far. I looked around for an entrance to the underground, realizing that what I thought was the entrance when I was back at the Eiffel Tower was really just part of the Louve itself.

Then I heard a distant click and the glass triangle exploded, sending shards of glass everywhere. I flew backward, trying to cover my eyes from the glass everywhere. For a quick second I saw a shard fly into one man's eye, blowing half of his head away, leaving a trail of blood and slick brain residue. Everything seemed to go in slow motion. Glass was everywhere, and as I flew I tucked my head into my chest, putting my arms around it. Glass cut everywhere; it seemed that every microsecond I felt a really annoying pinch on my arms. I felt some on my legs too, but it seemed that my jeans were offering some protection.

Then it ended and I slammed into the ground. I uncovered my eyes, seeing everyone on the ground, and blood everywhere. People were screaming, but the sounds felt distant. The skin on my face burned like a million suns and there was a buzzing in my head. I could not look five feet to the side without seeing a body missing a limb, with blood spurting out of the hole. Dust was everywhere, and I blinked as hard as I could to get it out of my eyes. Everyone was on the ground, trying to recover. I wondered if I could taste the radioactive bits in the air, but I knew that Robert, considering the fact that he had the bomb on him, had soaked it all in. I heard screams everywhere, but one scream was louder than the rest.

I slowly got up and started to make my way toward the destroyed triangle, no longer a triangle, but now an empty hole in the ground surrounded my shards of glass. I made my way to the edge, and looked down.

What I saw was not only glass everywhere, but tons of bodies, people that the shock wave had killed. Some were decapitated, sending a river of blood out of their neck. Others had half or even a quarter of head remaining, with blood and whatever remained of their brain hanging out of the hole. I resisted the urge to throw up and made my way to a staircase that used to go from the bottom to a door on the right side of the triangle.

I stepped over bodies, trying to avert my eyes away from the blood-soaked ground. I started to walk down the steps, glass everywhere, happy I was wearing shoes. My hearing was starting to return to normal, but still things sounded a bit distant. I looked down, all the stores that surrounded the area where the triangle used to be had all of the glass windows destroyed, all of the products thrown around. The dead were everywhere, and as I moved down behind me I could make out some noises of people trying to get up, and the sounds of an ambulance in the background, still sounding a bit distant.

The gun that I had been holding in my right hand had flown out in the blast, when I took flight to the air. I took the gun out of my left pocket as I walked down the steps, and realized that this was my last gun. I opened it up and checked the ammo, I was full with about six or seven bullets, I could not tell.

When I got to the bottom of the step, I stood in the spot where once people told one another to meet. The ground was littered with tiles, some that were once stuck into the ground providing a walkway now thrown around, revealing the sand underneath. Destruction was everywhere. I looked for the snarling demon version of Robert, but he was nowhere to be found. I held out the gun in front of me, listening for anything besides the screaming and crying above. But underground there was no noise, everyone was dead.

Tears started to go down my cheek and blood raced down my arms from the cuts of the flying glass when I realized that I had failed. I did not stop the bombing. All the dead people that I saw everywhere, it was entirely my fault. I tried to tell myself that I did try my hardest, that I sprinted my hardest, I looked my hardest for him, and at least I was not still at the Eiffel Tower wondering what the skup that boom and shaking of the ground was. I had tried my hardest. Now I had a new goal: stop the demon Robert from infecting anyone else. That meant killing him, and killing him fast. But first I had to find him.

I looked into the remnants of the stores from where I was, not moving my feet, just my eyes. Everywhere I looked I saw was the same thing: broken glass and dead bodies everywhere. Where the skup was he? One kitchen store had pots and pans thrown

around, along with some cutting knives, the big
butcher kind. I saw a dead employee on the ground,
one of the knives had flown out of its case and into her
forehead, blood dripping down.

I moved my gaze to a candy store. Candy and
wrappers were everywhere, mixing in with the broken
glass. There were also dead employees, killed by the
busted glass doors that people had once walked
through to come inside. Then I heard a screech behind
me.

"Robert, I know that you are there. Now come
out nice and easy," I said, eyes locked to wherever he
could be.

"MEEEELLLLLLVVVVVVVVIIIIIIIIINNNNNNNNN!" I
heard an angry voice yell to my left. I looked, and saw
nothing but dead bodies and glass mixed in with tiles.

"Robert, where the skup are you! Where the
skup are you! Come out, you coward!" I screamed, my
anger rising.

"NNNNNNNEEEEEEEEEEVVVVVVVVVVVVVEEEEE
EEEEEEEERRRRRRRRRRRR!" He sounded like a snake, a
hiss added to every sound. But I could not put a

position to the screeching. It sounded like he was everywhere at once. Chris warned me that this demon was more powerful than the rest, maybe he was doing this, messing with my brain.

"Come out, you coward!" I screamed. There was silence. I know that I had reached him in a place, a dark selfish cocky place deep inside Robert Bellamy's heart, which transferred to the demon version of him.

Then something big and heavy smashed into my back, sending me flying to the ground. When my hand hit, I briefly felt the gun wiggle out of my fingers and I saw it slide across the floor, and finally being stopped by a piece of tile sticking up around five feet away.

My head smashed into the ground, and when I tried to lift it up, it only got thrown back into the floor by powerful hands behind me. I tried to fling back my arm to strike him, but moving quicker than no other man on earth; I felt a fast hand whip it back to the ground. This was no doubt the demon Robert, more powerful than any demon that I have ever faced, and will ever face. This was it. My final battle

Chapter 12

When my one arm hit the ground, I struck out with the opposite, hitting something that resembled flesh. The thing screeched and let go of my arms. I remembered the move I had used on the "Eiffel Tower man" less than an hour ago, and I did the same here. I lifted up my left arm, and pushed it against him, sending him rolling over me. He rolled and fell to the tiles to the right of me. I quickly tried to get up, but the demon's foot came out of nowhere and smashed me in the chest, sending me sliding back. This one was fast, and strong, I had slid a good ten feet with one kick.

I looked at the demon. It was a horrible sight. He had blood dripping out of his mouth, boils all over his face, his forehead now a battlefield of sores and muscle. His arms were bigger than before, muscle taking up everything, even his legs were beefy. What the skup had I gotten myself into?

I looked past him and saw my gun around three feet behind him. I knew that the gun would not kill him, but at least it would slow him down. I had to get around him, but how? Since he was burly, didn't that also make him slow? No, real-life rules do not apply here. He was highly radioactive. That was another thing that did not make sense. Why wasn't I glowing in the dark? Why wasn't I growing an extra arm or eye? He must have used a new kind of radioactive bomb, a special kind. Either way, I had to escape from this demon.

How could I get around him? He was already getting up, anger flashing in his eyes. I was so skupped. I looked to my left and saw a piece of tile, a small broken shard. I picked it up and threw it at the beast while I tried to get up. It smashed him in the check, sending a small string of blood flying. The thing screeched, and I stood up. The thing ran toward me; spit flying out of his mouth.

I dove out of the way as the thing continued running, hitting a pole that used to hold up the glass triangle. I got out of the ball that I had turned myself into when I had smashed into the ground, and started to run toward the gun.

But before I could get close to the gun, the thing smashed into me again. We hit the ground then slid a couple feet, and I watched my gun get farther away. I adjusted myself and punched it in the face twice, once with each hand. It screeched and tried to hit me, but I pushed aside the hand before it could strike me. I needed to get to my gun.

I brought up my foot into its chest, trying to push it back. My foot was pushing against pure muscle, and as I tried to push it away it only slid half as fast as I wanted it to. It screeched and tried to get me with its waving fists, but I had pushed it too far away for it to touch me. It was now as far away as I could ever get it, so I released my foot and got up quickly, trying to make my way to the gun.

But the thing grabbed my ankle and tried to pull me back. I fell back down to the ground, and I stretched out my arm as far as I could, trying to reach the gun with my hand, but it was slightly too far. I stretched out my fingers, and my middle finger just touched the tip of the gun. So with one foot being held onto by the demon, and my other foot kicking it, I slowly guided my middle finger on top of the gun, slowly dragging it to me. When it was within reach I picked it up with my right hand, gave the demon one more kick, then brought around the gun and fired.

The thing's head got slammed by the bullet, blood bursting like water when a rock hits a puddle. I had shot it in the forehead, and I saw the flattened bullet now on the ground, it would never enter the thing's head. I emptied six more bullets into its head, it screaming in response. Blood poured out, but the thing was still alive. I threw the gun at its head, and started to crawl then run away as it held its forehead with both hands.

I had one destination: the kitchen store. As I ran in, I could hear the thing getting up behind me. I had to hurry as fast as I could. When I ran inside over all of the broken glass, I picked up what I needed: one of the fallen butchers' knives. I picked it up and wiped the dust off of it. I heard the thing approaching from behind, so I gripped the wooden handle tight.

I turned and jammed the knife in the thing's abdomen. It was still wearing what remained of a suit and red tie, but the knife went right through them and started mixing in blood with the red tie. I knew that I did not have time to make just the stomach suffer. I quickly took the knife out of its stomach and sliced its face, adding to the blood coming out of its mouth. A scar would make its home on the thing's face soon, but I would make sure that it did not live until then.

It screeched and I jabbed the knife into its chest, and it fell backward, smashing its head on top of a countertop before coming to rest on the floor. I automatically jumped to it, putting one knee on either side of his fallen body, making it so that he could not get up. I then brought the knife down into his chest, then pulling it back up with a string of blood attached, and then the blood fell back into the wound. I stabbed him two more times, the demon screeching in response. I jabbed the knife into its left arm, making sure that it could hit me with that arm and fist no more. I moved the knife around, trying to cut all of the nerves inside its body. I could see deep inside of its arm, and the dark red string things were the things that I had to cut. Once I would cut one then the demon would scream in response.

Then I felt and saw a big string of nerve inside the thing's arm, and I put both hands on the knife and cut it off. But when I realized that I had taken my right arm off of the thing's right arm, it was too late. I had left it armed. The thing brought up its fist and smacked me straight in the face, sending me flying over to the left. I hit my back on a counter, and stopped sliding. My back ached from the tough wooden counter. I massaged my temple with my two index fingers as the thing stood up, its left arm completely falling off, smashing into the ground and sending a spatter of blood onto the tiles.

I quickly looked around for the knife, and found it back where the demon was, it was right next to its right foot. I had to get to that blood-covered knife. The one-armed demon started to walk toward me, blood spurting out of the hole where the left arm was once attached. I looked around me quickly and saw a chunk of tile next to me. I picked it up and threw it at the beast; it glazed the thing's head, and gave me no reaction.

I stayed seated, knowing that if I got up it would only tackle me to the ground again. As it walked over I looked for another knife that may have fallen out of its metal case, but they were all in the back right corner of the store, and I was near the front left corner. I could not get a knife to defend myself. I picked up another chunk of tile and threw it at him, with no reaction. When he got close enough to me he kicked me once, making me feel the power of his burly legs.

I pulled myself into the fetal position as he kicked me again. I tried to cover up my stomach and chest with my arms, so that it wouldn't knock the air out of my lungs. When he kicked me hard enough for me to turn over, my head was stopped before hitting the ground by a rock that most likely flew in from outside. I took out one arm from around my chest and stomach and picked up the rock. It was shaped like a square on one side, but when I turned it over I saw that the other side was nice and sharp.

The beast kicked me again, and I dropped the rock. I picked it up again and turned around quickly and jabbed the sharp side into the thing's leg. Blood burst out and the thing screamed out in pain. I hit the wound with the rock again, this time scraping the rock down its leg, and making a cut all the way down its leg, with blood slowly coming out.

It screamed and I rolled to the right, behind the counter. I quickly recovered my speeding breath, and tried to steady my sprinting heart. I heard the thing bumping against the counter in pain, sending the dust that was once on the top raining down on me. I covered my eyes and started to crawl toward the knives that were in the corner, moving diagonally across the store.

I heard a giant crash behind me and I looked to see that the demon had pushed over the counter, and was now painfully limping toward me. I needed to prove that crawling was faster than limping as I crawled as fast as I could. When I got to the area where all of the knives were, I picked up the one nearest to me, aimed, and threw it behind me at the beast.

It stuck into the thing's chest, and he pulled it out and threw it back at me angrily. I tried to dodge it, but it grazed my face, making me see a string of red in front of my eyes for a quick second before the knife stuck into the floor. I picked it back up and threw it at its injured leg, trying to slow the monster down. It stuck into the wound, and the thing stopped, screaming out in intense pain.

Behind him I could see that the rain was now falling through the hole where the glass triangle once was, and I could hear paramedics above me, not knowing of the battle happening beneath them.

I picked up the largest knife and stood up with the knife in my hand, feeling power. The thing looked up at me, screaming in pain, crouched over trying to massage its leg. I kicked it in the head, making it fall over. Once it hit the ground I could see in its eyes that it wanted to kill me, but it had to protect its leg.

I put both knees on top of its chest, where blood was soaking its way through knife wounds. I made an attempt to put my knees on its wounds, and it screamed in reaction. I took out the knife and stabbed it in the neck, blood exploding out. I was now completely soaked in blood, the Muse logo on my shirt hidden by red goo and my blue jeans now turned red. The blood continued to burst out, like a cannon shooting out a cannon ball.

Why wasn't the thing dead yet? It continued to scream out in pain, its own blood going onto its face and making it choke. It was too strong for that. How did I kill the demons in the future when I went? I did beat one to death, but I already knew that this thing's body was too burly, I wouldn't be able to hit past the big muscles.

Then I remembered the one demon crying on the ground, what did I do to finally kill it? I had throw down the heel of my sneaker into its eye, and then pushing deep down until it had stopped moving. Could that work now? There was only one way to find out.

"This is going to be messy," I said mostly to myself, and hung the knife in air for a couple of seconds.

I saw a brief look of sadness on the beast's face, but then I quickly brought down the knife. It slammed into the thing's eyes, which instantly exploded, wet globs of pieces of the eyes slammed into my cheeks and face, but I kept the knife down. Blood burst out as the thing shook as if it has just been struck by a taser. It shook and shook, but I kept the knife down into its eye, moving it around, trying to get as deep as I possibly could to kill it.

It started to scream a scream that I have never heard before, it killed my ears from the deep inside. I resisted the urge to cover my ears, and just continued to push the knife deep inside. Blood was still spurting out, going everywhere and not just a liquid either, there were warm chucks of an unknown substance flying around, and being mixed in.

Then the thing stopped shaking, and everything went silent. Blood stopped flying out, everything seemed to stop. I heard footsteps coming down the stairs behind me, someone was finally coming down. I slowly got up from the dead body, with a seeming red black hole for a right eye. It was still as I walked over, and stopped behind the counter. What I saw were three men in suits with F.B.I. badges on. I must look like a monster with the cuts all over my body with blood slowly seeping out. The men walked inside of the store.

"Its OK guys, I'm on the good side," I said, flashing my best smile.

"We all know that is not true, Melvin, so cut the crap." The one in the middle said, looking at me while wearing dark sunglasses.

"What do you mean? Robert Bellamy was the bad one, he planned all of this!" I said quickly.

"No Melvin, we know about your secret." He said. I gasped, how could they know? How could they ever know? Did they look through the files? Did they ask the other F.B.I. man that caught me that one day? I thought I killed that man! What is going on! I still had the knife in my hand, but the men were pointing handguns at me. I needed to make a quick choice. Skup the law.

I threw the knife at the man, and saw blood burst out of his chest when it hit and I fell behind the counter as bullets flew over me. When I hit the ground, I knew that I had no time to waste. I quickly took out the items in my pocket, the ones from the electrical store. The men continued to shoot at me from the other side, but they were aiming too high. The bullets would go through the counter and over me. Doesn't every F.B.I. agent know that when someone is behind something to always aim low so that you hit them? Who were these men? Where they really F.B.I.?

I attached the wires that I had to attach, and pressed the buttons that needed to be pressed. Then I attached the final wire to the two units and typed the date on the mini keyboard that I needed to go to. I said goodbye to the men in my head and pressed the button. I instantly disappeared out of the store and dropped onto a beach in Ireland, 1980. It was time to try this life again, use a different name again and in a different country. I had cheated death again.

And he would come back for revenge.

Made in the USA
Lexington, KY
02 May 2011